Dead Girl's Diary

K. R. Alexander

Scholastic Inc.

If you purchased this book without a cover, you should be aware that this book is stolen property. It was reported as "unsold and destroyed" to the publisher, and neither the author nor the publisher has received any payment for this "stripped book."

Copyright © 2024 by Alex R. Kahler writing as K. R. Alexander

All rights reserved. Published by Scholastic Inc., *Publishers since 1920.* SCHOLASTIC and associated logos are trademarks and/or registered trademarks of Scholastic Inc.

The publisher does not have any control over and does not assume any responsibility for author or third-party websites or their content.

No part of this publication may be reproduced, stored in a retrieval system, or transmitted in any form or by any means, electronic, mechanical, photocopying, recording, or otherwise, without written permission of the publisher. For information regarding permission, write to Scholastic Inc., Attention: Permissions Department, 557 Broadway, New York, NY 10012.

This book is a work of fiction. Names, characters, places, and incidents are either the product of the author's imagination or are used fictitiously, and any resemblance to actual persons, living or dead, business establishments, events, or locales is entirely coincidental.

ISBN 978-1-339-01217-9

10 9 8 7 6 5 4 3 2 1   24 25 26 27 28

Printed in the U.S.A.   40
First printing 2024

Book design by Maithili Joshi

FOR THE AVID READERS...
WHO KNOWS WHAT STORIES AWAIT?

O

Written words are powerful.

Words can change your mood from happy to sad, or make you laugh on the darkest day. They can transport you anywhere—absolutely anywhere.

They can change your life.

Just like Elizabeth's diary changed mine.

I never could have guessed how much that little book would change everything. *Ruin* everything.

When it showed up at my house, I thought it was a prank. Kids were always pranking me. That's what you get when you're not cool or popular.

But when I started reading, I knew it was no joke. At least, there was nothing in those pages to laugh about. The girl in the diary sounded so familiar—she was bullied like I was, felt alone like I did. I felt like I knew her.

Probably because I'd had visions of her long before that diary ever showed up.

Visions of her in trouble. Visions of her trying to escape something terrible.

She was never able to escape.

By the time the diary showed up, I was sure Elizabeth was long dead.

That's why I knew I had to find out what had happened to her. Even though it meant leaving everything I knew behind. Even though I knew it might put me in the path of whatever terrible fate had befallen her. I had to know. I had to know the truth.

Elizabeth's words had changed my life.

How could I have known that her words might end my life, too?

"What are you reading, nerd?"

Megan's voice cuts through my story just as her hand swipes it away. I jolt and look up; she stands there, scoffing, as she thumbs through the pages of my book. Her expression turns wicked and I feel my cheeks flush.

"Really, Kara?" she taunts. "Horses? Aren't you a little old to be reading a book about horses?"

I don't say anything. She knows I won't say anything. Partly because a small, shamed part of me wonders if she's right. I'm twelve. Other girls my age aren't reading stories about horses. Or at least, I don't think they are. Except for my friend Sienna, I don't know if other girls my age are reading at all. You'd have to be friends with other girls to know that.

Megan tosses the book at my chest, and I catch it clumsily.

"Once a nerd, always a nerd," she says as she walks

away. She almost sounds like she feels bad about it, too. Like she's ashamed *for* me.

I watch her go. She wanders over to some other girls on the swing set across the playground. They all start laughing after she whispers to them. Laughing, and then pointing at me. I feel my cheeks flush all over again and bury my face in my book. Not that I can read it now. The words swim from the tears I refuse to cry.

It takes me a good ten seconds before I realize I'm holding the open book upside down.

Thankfully, a few moments later, Sienna saves me.

"Did Her Majesty of Meanies say something rude?" she asks. She sits down on the bench beside me.

"The usual," I reply. I hold up the novel. "She made fun of my book."

"Probably because it's way above her reading level," Sienna says.

Sienna looks to Megan and her friends. They've already forgotten all about me. Trouble is, I know I won't forget about what Megan said for a while. Rude comments are like that—they stick.

"You're going to have to learn how to stand up for yourself," Sienna says. "I can't always be around."

She says it kindly, gently. But it stings, too.

Sienna is my best and only friend. She's shorter

than me and plays softball and is in theater, and even though she isn't really popular, she's not picked on, either. She just has an attitude, a presence, that intimidates even the meanest of bullies. Which is funny, because she's really sweet and nice and gentle. Once, she even nursed a baby bird that fell from its nest back to health.

Also, she's the one who gave me the horse book. She has the full series.

I wish I could be like her.

I'm taller, and I play soccer, but in spite of that, everyone still picks on me. I want to say I don't know why, but I do.

I'm . . . different.

I always have been. And no matter how hard I try, I can't make that difference go away.

Sienna picks up on my mood and puts a hand on my shoulder.

"But I'm around now," she says with a big grin. She tilts her head to the side like a creepy doll. "And we'll be best friends forever and ever and ever."

That makes me laugh. I push her gently.

"On that thought, maybe I'd be better off with Megan as my friend," I tease. Sienna just sticks out her tongue.

She pulls out her own book, and we spend the rest

of lunchtime recess reading together and occasionally sharing our favorite parts. She's reading a book about space pirates—that was from my personal library—and she keeps gasping or yelping when exciting things happen. Kids keep looking our way, but Sienna doesn't pay them any mind.

I try my best to mirror her carefree attitude. I even let myself gasp. Quietly. Once.

When the bell rings, we pack up and begin heading inside.

I'm a few steps toward the door when the whole world *tilts*.

I wobble as the school goes sideways, as the breeze that was billowing around me slows and then freezes. I don't move. Can't move. Can't look around at the other kids frozen in time, can only barely see Sienna's smiling face from the corner of my eye.

Until, a second later, I snap free.

My body jolts, and the moment it does, the world shifts, blurs, like I'm the only thing able to move, and then it's no longer the school I see but somewhere else.

A large, empty house stands against the stark sky. Broken white shutters. Peeling yellow paint. A gaping front door, like a dislocated jaw. Tangled weeds choking the lawn.

And coming from the house I've seen a

hundred times in these visions, a voice. A voice I've heard a hundred times as well.

Only this time, it says more than my name. It says something new.

"Kara," the girl's voice calls. "Kara, you're in danger."

Something moves in an upstairs window. A figure.

A little girl . . .

Reality snaps back, and I stumble on the steps and nearly fall to the ground. I would have if Sienna hadn't steadied me. A few other kids chuckle, thinking I just tripped. Megan is one of them.

I don't pay them any attention, and not because I'm suddenly brave like Sienna.

No, my heart is racing in my chest and fear pulses like sickness in my veins. It takes all my concentration not to throw up.

I'm in danger?

"Are you okay?" Sienna asks.

I barely hear her over the blood pounding in my ears. My hands shake. If I don't sit down soon, my whole body will start to shiver. It happens every time I have one of my visions.

I've been having them more frequently.

"Was it . . . another one?" she asks, quieter.

I nod. She's the only person who knows. Everyone else thinks I'm just scared of my own shadow or something, and have panic attacks because of it.

"Let's get you inside," she says. She keeps a firm hold on my arm so I don't collapse, and guides me into the school.

I know she continues talking to me. Trying to soothe me. Telling me it will all pass.

I don't hear her.

Because behind me, a hundred miles away in a town I've never visited, I can still hear the ghost girl calling my name.

2

I've always had visions.

Sometimes, I think my earliest memories *are* those visions. Because they surely aren't my memories at all.

I remember walking down a long hallway with faded orange carpet and family photos looking down at me. It wasn't my family, and it wasn't my house.

I remember playing ball with a neighborhood boy. I swear I'd never seen him before in my life.

I remember playing video games and watching movies. But I've never owned those consoles, and I've never seen those movies.

As I sit on the bus home, staring out the window, all I can think about is that large house with the tangled yard and the empty windows. In the beginning, I only had visions of it maybe once every couple of months. Then, in the last year, I've seen it more frequently. Every month. Every week.

And now, every day.

It's seared into my mind, so much so that when the

bus stops outside my *real* house, I almost don't get off, almost don't recognize that this is where I'm supposed to be.

At least until Megan throws a wadded-up piece of paper at me and I jerk back to reality.

"Earth to Kara," Megan says sarcastically. She turns back to her friend. "She's so *weird*."

I ignore the blush in my cheeks and hurry to the front of the bus, past the snickering kids and the bus driver, who looks at me with a raised eyebrow. I don't look back as the bus pulls away.

It's strange, but when I stare up at my house, it almost feels like someone else's, just for a moment. The fresh blue paint, the neatly mowed lawn (my mom mows twice a week), the perfect flowers in the raised beds. It's such a stark contrast to the house in my visions, and it *should* be welcoming. After all, that's the driveway where I learned how to ride my bike. That's the front porch where I broke an umbrella because I leaped off thinking I'd fly away like Mary Poppins. I have so many memories of this place . . . and yet, when I turn my head, I fully expect my vision to tilt again, for the colors to fade to gray and be replaced with an empty, abandoned home.

I don't understand why I almost *want* that to happen. I grew up here. I was born in this town.

So why do I feel like I'm part of somewhere *else*?

I make my way inside and am nearly bowled over by our mastiff, Brutus. He's easily three times my size and slobbers like a broken faucet. Most people are afraid of him because he's so huge, but I open my arms wide when he stampedes toward me and covers me in sloppy, wet kisses. Appearances aren't always the truth, and Brutus is a great example of that.

"Down, boy, down," I say, wiping his slobber off my face.

He sits immediately, a goofy smile on his face.

"Do you need to go outside?"

He immediately does a spin, and I laugh again. Walking him when I get home has become one of my chores, but I like it more than all the others, like washing the dishes or vacuuming the living room. I drop my bag on the floor and clip his leash to his collar, checking the mail on the way out—some bills for Mom and Dad, nothing for me. Then we go for a walk.

It's a nice day, and Brutus doesn't pull on his leash, so my mind wanders.

Of course, it wanders back to the vision. To the empty house.

To the girl's voice.

xxx

Years ago, when I learned that not everyone had visions like mine, I told my parents about them. Mom gasped, and Dad looked like he'd seen a ghost. They asked me all about what I'd seen (at the time, it had just been the abandoned house) and then demanded I tell them if I ever had another vision again.

For some reason, their insistence scared me more than the visions. I never told them about it again.

They'll ask, every once in a while, and I'll lie and say I don't know what they're talking about. I hate not telling them the truth, but something warns me that if I told them just how many visions I have, things would get a lot worse.

I only told Sienna because—a few years after we became friends—the visions started causing me to shake, and she was worried about me. I had to tell her the truth. Plus, by that point, I knew I could trust her with my life. We'd already told each other all our little secrets.

Unlike when I told my parents, when I told Sienna about my visions, she got excited. She said I should start writing them down in a diary. I never did—mostly for fear of what my parents would say if they found it.

Since then, I've learned to control the shivering. Mostly. But I can't control when the visions happen.

I'm also not any closer to understanding *why* they happen. Maybe I should have taken Sienna's advice and written them all down.

Usually, they're only a few seconds long. A house. A hallway. A glimpse. Sometimes I hear voices, like kids playing or parents calling out. Once, I heard a scream.

Never has a voice said I was in danger.

But danger from *what*? I've never seen anything more than that creepy house, and I don't even know where it is. I've tried researching it before. With Sienna's help. We spent all afternoon one Saturday (when we were supposed to be doing homework) trying to find the house from my visions. It was in vain—turns out, there are a lot of old yellow houses in the Midwest. We gave up after looking at the millionth house on a real estate website and started looking up Sienna's favorite K-pop group instead. After that, we gave up.

I soon realize that I'm home. I've somehow managed to do my entire loop, and Brutus is panting beside me. I shake my head—it's bad enough I have visions, but I can't start losing track of time like that, too.

As I make my way up to the steps, Brutus starts to growl.

Goose bumps break out over my skin. Brutus never growls or barks. Not even at the mailperson or skateboarders. Mom always jokes that he's the worst guard dog. Now I'm not so sure. He's downright scary.

I look around, but there's no one hiding in the yard—not that we have bushes to hide in, or anywhere to hide on the porch.

The porch.

There's something there.

A small package. About the size of a book. It looks old-fashioned, wrapped in brown paper and tied with string.

I edge a little closer. Brutus growls louder.

"It's just a package," I tell him. My dad likes collecting rare books. It's probably for him.

I finally convince Brutus to follow, though his growls turn to whimpers and his tail tucks between his legs when we near.

"Why are you acting so strange?" I ask him. "It's just a—"

But the words catch in my throat when I look down.

It *is* just a package. A plain, simple package.

Except it isn't addressed to Dad.

It's addressed to me.

3

I call Sienna over the moment I've fed Brutus dinner. Mom and Dad still aren't home by the time she arrives—she only lives a few blocks away and biked over immediately.

"What do you think it is?" she asks.

The package sits between us on my bed, still unopened.

"I don't know," I reply. "A book? But who would send me a book without a return address?"

"And without postage," she says.

"Wait, what?"

She rolls the package over. My name and address are on the front in handwriting I don't recognize, but she's right—there's no postage.

"So how did it get here?" I ask.

She hesitates, then says, "Do you think someone left it on your porch? When you weren't here?"

"You mean like they were spying on me?"

She shrugs. "Maybe. You were only gone for like

twenty minutes, right? Seems awfully convenient."

"But why?"

"Maybe they didn't want you to know who it was. It would explain why there's no return address."

She hands the package back over to me, and my hands shake when I take it. The package feels heavy, heavier than it should. And cold. As if it contains a brick of ice. I tell myself it's my overactive imagination, but that doesn't help.

"I almost don't want to open it," I say.

"It'll be fine," she replies. Then, softer, "Probably."

I raise an eyebrow. "That doesn't make me feel any better."

"Oh, quit stalling and open it."

I take a deep breath and slowly, gingerly—as if I'm trying to preserve the paper—unwrap it.

I quickly learn three things.

> One: It's definitely a book of some sort. It looks like a journal. A diary.
>
> Two: It's definitely not new. The leather cover is worn and stained.
>
> Three: Even though I could swear I've never seen it before, a part of me recognizes it immediately.

My hands caress the cover almost of their own

free will. It feels like cool electricity fizzes over my fingers as they do. And that sensation I get when my visions hit—that heavy thrumming in my eardrums, the slight wobble to my sight—comes back even stronger.

Only one word resonates in my mind:

mine.

"What is it?" Sienna asks, knocking me from my daydream.

"I . . . I dunno," I reply. And I don't. I've never seen or held this before. So why does a part of me think I have? Is this a new aspect of my visions? "It looks like a diary or something."

"Can I?" Sienna asks, holding out a hand. I pass it over to her.

The moment I do, a part of me clenches, wants to grab it back. The instinct is so strong it scares me; it takes all my self-control not to grab the diary back from her the moment it leaves my hands.

Get ahold of yourself, I think angrily.

She examines the book. There's no lock or latch, just a long strip of dry leather wrapped around it a few times like string. She gently unrolls the leather binding. Then she opens it.

A moment passes.

Her eyebrows furrow.

She flips to the next page.

   And the next.

            And the next.

Her eyebrows scrunch tighter with every page.

My stomach scrunches tighter as well.

"What is it?" I ask. "What does it say?"

"I'm not sure," she replies. She shakes her head like she's shaking off a bad thought, then hands the diary over to me. "See for yourself."

I scan the page she's opened to.

Dec 4

James and I played pirates today, but he kept saying he was the captian, even though I have a better ARRR than him. He laffed when I said so. He can be so mean sometimes. But then we had ice cream after dinner and mom let me have two scoops so I'm not mad anymore.

I look up at Sienna. I open my mouth to speak, but she interjects.

"Weird, right?" she asks.

"Wha—"

She takes the diary back and rapidly flips through to the end.

"I mean, it's every page!" she says incredulously. "Who would fill an entire diary with this?"

With ordinary diary entries? I want to ask. But I don't, because my brain isn't quite catching up to what she's saying. I feel like she's pranking me, but I don't know why, or about what.

"What do you mean?" I finally manage.

She hands the diary back. "It's all gibberish," she says. "It's no language I've ever seen."

I look from her to the diary. The entry in front of me is plain as day.

Sept 23

It's so hot and I wish we had a pool. James has a pool but he won't let me swim in it because he's being a butt. Mom says I shouldn't say that word but he is and I am. I'm going to get him back. When it isn't so hot.

"Who would send you a diary filled with a made-up language?" Sienna ponders.

I don't know what to say.

I know that Sienna isn't messing with me—she isn't like Megan. She'd never do something like that.

Which means she's telling the truth: When she looks at the diary, she sees only gibberish.

When I look at it, I can read it perfectly.

I don't know what that means, but when I look back down at the book in my hands, I can only think one thing:

This is dangerous.

4

"So you can't read this?" I ask her.

"No," she says. "It looks like it's written in some sort of code." She looks at me funny. "Why . . . can you?"

For a moment I consider lying. I can't explain what's happening right now, and I don't want her to think I'm making it up. Then again, I couldn't explain my visions, either, and she never doubted them. If there's anyone I can rely on in this world to believe me, it's Sienna.

I nod.

"Seriously?" she asks.

"Yeah," I say. "It looks like normal words to me."

She shakes her head in disbelief. "That doesn't make any sense."

"I know."

"Do you think it might have to do with your visions?"

"I don't know. Maybe?"

"Does it say whose diary it is?" she asks.

I flip to the first page. Sure enough, it shows the author.

Property of Elizabeth Townsend

"Elizabeth," I say. "Elizabeth Townsend."

"Never heard of her. Have you?"

"No."

Sienna sighs. "So she doesn't live around here. I don't think anyone in town even has that last name. I wonder why someone left it for you?"

"I don't know," I say.

"Maybe you should read more. See if you can find any clues."

"Okay . . ."

I'm about to start reading the next page when a knock at my bedroom door makes me yelp. I quickly snap shut the diary and look up, just as my mom comes in.

"Hi, Sienna," Mom says. "I saw your bike out front. Are you staying for dinner? I was going to order pizza."

"Oh, sure," Sienna says. "I'd love to."

"What's that?" Mom asks, looking at the diary.

"A present," Sienna quickly answers. "I found it at the antique store and thought Kara would like it."

"How sweet." Mom looks at her watch. "Well, I'll get that pizza ordered and have your dad pick it up. Why don't you girls come down and work on your homework before dinner?"

I want to push back, to stay here and finish reading, but I know that would just get me in trouble. So I tuck the diary under my pillow and grab my books. Together, Sienna and I head to the kitchen table to do some work.

The entire time, all I can think about is Elizabeth's diary.

Normally, I'd be super excited that Sienna was able to stay for dinner, and that we were having pizza. But when Mom brings out the ice cream, I immediately think of that diary entry I read, about getting ice cream. It makes me want to go up and read the diary even more than I did before.

Sienna can't stay after dinner, so she makes me promise to read the diary and tell her all about it. When she goes, I tell my parents I'm going to go read and head to my room. Thankfully, this isn't unusual for me, so they aren't suspicious.

Finally I'm alone.

Finally I can read it.

For a while, I don't actually open it. I just examine the cover, turning it this way and that, letting my fingers toy with the long leather string that keeps it bound shut. The more I stare at it, the more familiar it feels. The more *right* it feels to have it in my possession.

Once more, my vision seems to blur a little around the edges, as though my real world and my fantasy world are becoming one.

I read.

Aug 17

Mom got me a new diary. She says it's so I can right down all the exciting things that happen in our town. I think it's to distract me from how boring it is.

Nothing ever changes. I hate it.

But there is always James. He lives down the block, and I guess he's my friend. He isn't always friendly, though. A few days ago, he wanted to play hide-and-seek together. The next day, he made fun of my shirt. Today, he brought me candy.

I don't understannd him. But he's the only friend I have.

The next entry is similar.

Aug 22

James came over to play today. I was playing with dolls. He said they were girly and brought out his toy soldiers. His soldiers fought my dolls. He was mean. James even pulled the head off poor Kelly.

I cried.

Our naybor Mr. Pierce came over. He lives a few blocks away. He is old and mean. I don't like him.

He said if I didn't stop crying he would give me a reason to cry. James ran away.

Mr. Pierce scares me.

I skim the next dozen or so pages. They aren't exactly interesting—updates on Elizabeth's life.

James and her playing. Wanting to leave town.

But then I realize that some of the pages have been torn out. It looks like five or ten pages near the end.

Why would someone rip them out? I wonder.

I skip to the last page to read the final entry and feel my blood run cold.

Feb 10

He is coming after me. He is going to hurt me.

If you are reading this, I want you to know

The rest of the page is ripped out, as if someone didn't want readers to know what happened next.

But behind it, on the next page, is a note. Folded and taped to the blank page. It feels like a clue.

I gently peel it out and unfold it. It's not just a piece of paper—it's a clipping from a newspaper.

It's not the heading that makes my blood run cold, though it's terrifying enough:

Elizabeth Townsend, 12, Drowned in Lake

It's the photo beside it.

A smiling girl with long brown hair and dimples and big, innocent eyes. A girl who looks like she should have her whole life ahead of her.

The owner of this diary.

The girl

from

my

visions.

5

Sleep is the last thing on my mind. I slip the diary into my nightstand and turn out the light, but I can't get my brain to quiet. I have a thousand questions about the diary and Elizabeth and my visions and why the diary was sent to me.

Does someone else know about what I see?

Who?

If I'm having visions of Elizabeth, are we linked somehow?

Is she haunting me?

I want to stay up all night reading the diary, trying to find answers. The trouble is, I know my parents will see the light on, so I have to force myself to lie there and wait for sleep to come.

Hours pass.

I hear my parents go to bed.

And finally, as my body starts to feel heavy and my brain starts to drift, I feel sleep sink in. The last conscious thought I have before drifting away is, *What's going on?*

xXx

I stand in front of the giant yellow house.

Only now, the house from my vision isn't broken down or empty. It looks brand-new.

The windows are open and white lace curtains billow out, while down in the yard, pristine rosebushes bloom with heavy red flowers. The porch is painted fresh white, a few rocking chairs swaying in the breeze. I turn around, taking in the cozy neighborhood with its picket fences and red fire hydrants, cars gleaming in the summer sun and sprinklers casting sprays of water over the neighbors' lawns. It looks like a postcard, except the people on the street are moving and waving and saying hello.

One walking couple passes right through me without noticing, and that's how I know I'm dreaming.

When I look back to the large yellow house, my feet start walking toward it without me moving them.

I think for a moment that I'm going to the front porch, but I don't stop there. I'm guided around the side of the house, toward a backyard filled with apple trees and hedges and a neat garden of corn and tomatoes.

A girl sits there, all alone, her back to a hedge and a book in her hands.

No, a diary.

It's Elizabeth.

I walk closer. I can almost see what she's writing. Her tongue sticks out a little as she concentrates.

I figure she'll ignore me like everyone else in the dream, but the moment my shadow falls over the page, she looks up.

Her eyes widen.

Her mouth opens in shock.

"*It's you,*" she and I say at the exact same time.

The dream shifts.

Now I'm by a lake. Tall maples stretch up around it, the water brown and murky and covered in lily pads and reeds. I stand on the shore.

Elizabeth stands beside me.

"What are we doing here?" I ask. My voice sounds hollow.

She points. To the water.

I look.

I walk.

My feet press into the mud, squelch into the muck.

I don't want to go any farther.

Because there, hiding beneath the lily pads, I see shocks of white.

A dress.

Splayed hands.

A halo of brown hair.

Still, I walk closer.

I look over my shoulder.

Elizabeth is no longer there.

Elizabeth is right in front of me, bobbing beneath the water.

My feet finally pause. Water sweeps around my knees.

The body

turns

over

to reveal Elizabeth's poor face, splotchy and sad.

Dead.

Her eyes snap open.

I scream out.

Stagger back.

Fall and splash into the water.

She rises up in front of me.

She points back to the shore.

"He did this to me," she croaks. Her voice sounds like grating pebbles and bullfrogs.

She looks down at me.

I keep sinking into the water.

It slurps over my face,

pools in my mouth.

Lily pads blot out the sun.

Still, I hear her voice, as clear and terrible as thunder.

"He'll do this to you, too."

Then I sink deeper, and the lake swallows me whole.

6

When I wake up, my sheets are covered in cold sweat.

At least, I think it's sweat. A part of me can't help but notice it smells like pond water. I tell myself it's just my imagination and throw the sheets in the hamper.

I can't pay attention to my parents all through breakfast. Just like during dinner, all I can think about is the diary. But this time, I have another layer to the mystery—the nightmare.

I have no doubt that it was another vision. It felt just like the visions I've had my entire life. I've just never had them while asleep. I've also never really had proof that they are, well, *real*. But the diary proves it.

Elizabeth Townsend was a real girl. She wrote a diary of her life.

And then, one day, she drowned in a lake.

If the nightmare is anything to go by, it wasn't an accident.

But even though the last twenty-four hours have given me more answers than I ever thought I'd get about my visions, I now have even more questions.

Mainly: Why have I been having visions of Elizabeth my entire life? And who knew I'd been having them?

The questions run through my head all through breakfast, then it feels like I blink and I'm on the bus. I don't even remember hugging my parents goodbye. All I know is, the diary is safe in my backpack, and every single part of me would rather be home reading it over again, rather than going to a place where I'll be distracted from it all day.

I've always loved school, but with this mystery literally sitting in my lap, it just doesn't feel *important*.

I'm clearly not the only one who feels that way. Sienna is waiting for me when I get off the bus, and pulls me away from the other kids the moment my foot touches the ground.

"Did you bring it?" she whispers. She looks conspiratorial when she asks, but no one's paying attention.

A small perk of being a loser—*no one ever pays attention*. Unless it's Megan and she's trying to harass me.

"It's in my bag," I whisper back. "Why are we whispering?"

"I dunno," she says, and resumes her normal tone. "Did you read any more of it?"

"Yeah. And you'll never guess what I found."

Rather than tell her, I pull out the diary and show

her the newspaper article, which I safely tucked back inside. Her eyes go wide when she reads it.

"Who would send you a dead girl's diary?" she asks.

"It gets even weirder. I . . ." This time, I look around and drop my voice. "I had another vision. In my dreams. It was her. Elizabeth. And she said she hadn't drowned—she was murdered." I leave out the part about Elizabeth warning me that whoever killed her would try to kill me. Sienna would freak. Besides, something tells me that so long as I stay right here, I'll be fine. Elizabeth lived somewhere far, far away, after all.

Sienna stares at me for a long while. I realize then how fantastical that sounds. No one should believe what I've just said. For a moment, I worry she's going to burst into laughter, thinking I'm pulling her leg.

Instead, her eyebrows knit, and she drops her voice once more.

"Did she say who did it?" she asks.

"No. Just that it was a *he*."

"Then he could still be out there."

"Maybe. Or it could have been a hundred years ago. Who knows?"

"That newspaper clipping doesn't look a hundred years old. It looks pretty recent."

This is why I rely on Sienna—she sees the things I skip over.

I don't respond, and she bites her lip as she thinks.
"So what are you going to do?" she finally asks.
"I don't know," I tell her.

And that's the hardest part of all this: I know Elizabeth warned me away, but I need to know what happened to her. It feels like my life depends on it.

✗✗✗

Thankfully, Sienna isn't just my best friend—she loves a good detective story.

When lunchtime rolls around, she hands me a printout from the library with a satisfied smile.

"What's this?" I ask.

"A list of every drowning within two hundred miles," she says. "Miss Peters was a little concerned why I wanted to search for it, but I told her it was for a school project. I don't think she bought it, but who cares? I'd tried searching for the name, but there are like a million Elizabeth Townsends out there."

I pull the list closer. It's just a bunch of cities, but one of them is circled in highlighter.

"Is this . . . ?" I ask, leaning in.

"Yup," she replies. "After that search, I was able to cross-reference and found the newspaper article you had online. That's where Elizabeth Townsend lives. *Lived*."

"It's not that far," I say.

Only a hundred miles or so.

"Nope," she says. Her smile grows wider. "It also wasn't that long ago. Only like twelve years. You know what I'm thinking?"

I look at her, the tiny bubble of hope in my chest popping. A hundred miles isn't *that* far, but it's still *too* far when neither of us can drive, or really do anything without our parents' permission.

"Yes," I say. "But we can't."

"Oh, come on. Just for the weekend. I already found a bus that will take us right there."

"But our parents—"

"Will never know. I thought of that, too. We can tell your parents that you're invited to a camping trip with my family. Somewhere with no service. And I'll tell my parents the same, but that it's with your family."

"They'll never buy that."

"Sure, they will!" Sienna replies. "When have you ever done anything wrong?"

I pause.

She has a point.

I've never put a toe out of line. Never. My parents trust me so much that I haven't had a babysitter lately, and they've stopped telling me when to be home when I go to Sienna's because they know I'll be back on time no matter what. They trust me. They trust her.

And if we do this and they find out, they'll never trust either of us again.

It makes my stomach hurt.

Before I can say yes or no, however, my vision tilts.

I'm back in front of the yellow house. Empty. Abandoned. Frightening.

So why don't I want to run away?

Mist swirls on the path before me, forms the shape of a young girl.

Elizabeth.

She doesn't speak. She just holds out her hand, and I can't tell if she's warning me away or trying to invite me closer. Her mouth opens . . .

"Well?" Sienna asks. My vision shatters.

"What?" I reply.

"Are you in? It's Thursday, so we'd have to tell our parents like today if we're going to do it."

"I . . ."

My stomach clenches.

"I'll have to think about it," I say.

She sighs heavily, but she doesn't push it.

"Tonight, then," she says.

I don't answer. I just poke at my food, though eating is the last thing on my mind.

How can I focus on food when I feel so haunted?

7

My decision is made for me when the final bell rings. And it's made by the one person I dislike the most in the world.

Megan.

I'm gathering my books at my locker, and for a brief moment I pause to cast a secretive look at the diary, which is still folded up in an old T-shirt. Megan approaches from behind without making a sound.

"What are you hiding, nerd?" she asks.

Before I can stop her, she yanks the diary from my hands and opens it.

I don't even yelp at her not to do it. I'm too scared of what she might do if I fight back.

I watch helplessly as her eyes go from delight to confusion.

"What is this?"

"It's—"

"Look at this garbage," Megan says, skimming the

pages. She looks at me. "Did you do all this yourself? Some sort of secret code for other freaks?"

"It's . . . It's not . . ."

"Speak up, freak!" Megan says. "Are you writing mean things about us in your diary? Is that it?"

She shakes the diary in front of me, getting aggressive as she makes herself angry.

"I'm not—it isn't—"

Then the newspaper article falls out.

It flutters to the ground innocently. Megan stoops down to pick it up.

"What's this?" she asks.

She tucks the diary under her arm and unfolds the article. Her eyes go wide.

"What is *wrong* with you?" Megan asks. "Why would you save an article about a dead girl? You're such a freak, you know that? Freak!"

She drops the article and the diary to the ground as she walks away, calling out "Freak!" every few steps. She even stops to whisper to passing students, so by the time I've gathered my things, everyone in the hall is staring at me and whispering. A few girls in the corner giggle.

Sienna pushes through the crowd, looking curiously at everyone who's looking at me.

"What's going on?" she asks. The moment she's

there, the crowd starts to disperse. But I know that by tomorrow morning, everyone in school will have another reason to make fun of me. They'll all think that I'm obsessed with dead people, that I keep a diary of gibberish and am making mean notes. None of which are true.

Tears fill my eyes.

"I'll do it," I say. My voice is rough.

"What?"

"I'll go. We're going. Tomorrow."

"But tomorrow's still a school day."

"I don't care," I say. "We'll skip. No one will notice."

I look to where Megan is still gossiping with some older kids. When she sees me looking at her, she smiles. I don't tell Sienna the truth. That I'm scared to show up here tomorrow, that I can't stand the thought of showing my face when I've been humiliated. Again.

I'd rather face Elizabeth's ghost than Megan's rumors.

"I have to know what happened to Elizabeth," I tell Sienna instead. *I have to prove to myself that I'm not what Megan says—a freak.*

✗✗✗

Sienna was right about one thing: My parents are quick to trust me.

I tell them over dinner that Sienna invited me to a last-minute camping trip, and that her family is leaving right after school tomorrow.

They don't ask questions.

My mom even helps me pack some camping gear we had in the garage. I don't bring much—I tell her that Sienna's parents have all the big stuff, like tents and sleeping bags—but I let her fill a backpack with a flashlight and emergency supplies and warm clothes. I don't know what to expect when we get to Elizabeth's town, but if she was murdered, I want to be prepared for anything.

I text with Sienna all night and we formulate our plan.

We're going to leave first thing in the morning. We'll sneak off to the bus station, and away we go. Sienna already managed to get the tickets, so we don't have to worry about being questioned. It's all sorted out.

I know I should feel bad. Guilty. I've never lied to my parents before, and now I'm not just lying to them— I'm putting myself in danger and not telling them about it. It's so unlike me, it feels like someone else is doing all the plotting and planning. At the same time, I know I can't stay here a moment longer. I can't keep being the girl with the visions. I can't keep being the laughingstock of the school. I have to know what's happening, and why. And I know that the only way to figure that out is to find out what happened to Elizabeth. She might be warning me away, but I know that her death and my visions and her diary are linked somehow. If I can solve one, I can solve all of it, and I'll finally be normal.

By the time I go to bed, everything is ready. The tickets, the timing, the cover stories. I have enough granola bars in my bag to last us a week. I curl up with the diary on my pillow beside me. I'm too tired to read any more entries.

"Tomorrow, I find out what happened to you," I whisper to the diary.

When sleep finally comes, I dream of large yellow houses and old men with threatening sneers.

8

Elizabeth's town looks almost identical to my own.

I don't know what I expected when we snuck onto the bus this morning. Maybe that we'd arrive in this new location and I would feel different, that my visions would come back stronger, or we'd step off the bus and the sky would be gray and stormy and everything would feel haunted and wrong.

But none of that's the case.

The town is small, maybe only a few thousand people. The houses all look like they could be in my neighborhood. It's almost a disappointment: My parents rarely take me on vacation, and we never drive to any nearby town. We've been to some major theme parks out of state, but it's hitting me how close this place was, yet we never considered coming here. I wonder if my parents have even heard about this place.

I poke Sienna awake when the bus stops at the station—she fell asleep halfway here, and I let her snore away. I couldn't sleep even if I wanted to. I was too excited. She snorts awake and looks around.

"Arewethere?" she slurs.

"Yeah," I say. "And you've got drool on your chin."

She wipes her chin as I grab my bag and exit the bus.

The day is sunny and warm, just as it was back home. Nothing eerie or ominous. The bus station is on the edge of a small main street that's filled with bustling shops and restaurants. Families and couples are out shopping or walking their dogs. If anything, the town feels *happier* than the place I just left behind.

"Are we in the right place?" I ask, watching a kid and his mom walk past, each of them eating ice cream cones. They smile at us as they pass. The kid even waves.

Weird. People back home barely even look at each other on the street.

"Yeah," Sienna says. "I quadruple-checked."

"But . . ." *This doesn't look like a place where bad things happen*, I want to say. But I catch myself. I watch the news; bad things can happen anywhere.

"I know," Sienna says, catching my drift.

"Where do we even start?" I ask. "Did you get an address?"

"No, just the town. But it's not that big. I figure we can just . . . ask around?"

Suddenly, I'm hit by the weight of what we've done. We're a few hours from home. No one knows we've left. We *skipped school*. And we have no clue what to do—who to talk to, where to start looking.

We don't even have anywhere to *sleep* tonight.

This all feels like a very bad idea.

I turn around. The bus is already gone from the station.

"Maybe we should see about a return," I venture.

I take a step toward the information booth.

But before I can chicken out of this adventure, my vision shifts.

The world crackles around the edges, becomes slightly grainy and blurry. I turn, everything around me frozen in time, and see a girl about my age standing on the sidewalk. Right where I'd been standing moments before.

Elizabeth.

She glows like a small sun.

What do I do? I want to ask.

"*You shouldn't be here,*" she responds.

But I have to be! I think. *I need to know what happened to you.*

She looks at me sadly. "*It's already too late for you. Now that you're here . . .*" She lowers her head. I see a single tear fall to the ground. She doesn't say anything else. Instead, she points.

My vision shifts *again*, ricocheting down the street like a chaotic bird in flight. Elizabeth now stands at this street corner, pointing another direction. Again and again my vision shifts, Elizabeth pointing the way each time, until it stops in front of the ruined house.

Then I blink, and I'm back to reality.

"What?" Sienna asks. "What is it?"

"Elizabeth," I say, relief plain in my voice. "She was pointing the way."

Another family walks past on the opposite sidewalk. They, too, look at us and smile and wave. I shudder.

"Well then," Sienna says. "Let's follow before you forget."

We trudge down the street, Elizabeth's directions clear in my mind. Even at the fourth and fifth intersection, I remember where she pointed as clear as day. It's almost as familiar as walking through my own neighborhood. Honestly, the way people are smiling and waving at us makes me feel like this *is* my neighborhood. Everyone we pass wishes us a good day, or compliments us somehow.

"Is it weirding you out how *nice* everyone is?" Sienna asks after a woman pushing a stroller asked if we needed help with directions. We said no, and she gave us a cheery grin and kept on. I swear even her baby smiled at us.

"Yeah," I reply. "I thought it was just me."

"Nope." She looks back toward the woman and the stroller. "Definitely not just you."

"I think I'd rather be back where no one notices me."

"Me too."

We keep walking. We do our best to avoid the attention of people on the street, but it's impossible. It feels like the whole town is out for an afternoon stroll, and everyone wants to say hello.

Finally, we're there.

And the house is exactly like it was in my visions.

"Are you sure this is it?" Sienna asks quietly. Though of course it is. I know it as sure as I know my own name.

"This is it," I say.

The house is two stories tall and faded yellow. Windows have been broken in, and others are boarded up. The front porch looks like it might collapse at any minute. The yard is overgrown with weeds. The sidewalk leading up to the front steps is cracked and tangled with vines and dandelions.

On either side of the vacant house, the homes are intact and welcoming—neat lawns, fresh paint, tidy gardens. Every house on the street is picture-perfect, which just makes this one look like even more of an eyesore. I don't know how or why anyone would let a house like this continue to exist in a neighborhood this nice. Why hasn't it been torn down? Why hasn't anyone fixed it?

What happened to Elizabeth's family? Did they leave? Did someone else move in after Elizabeth died?

The yellow house is entirely uninviting.

And yet, a small voice inside me whispers: *home.*

Sienna asks, "What do we do now?"

I look to her.

"This was your idea?" I say, more a question than a statement.

"Yeah, but you have the visions. I thought maybe being here would, I dunno, spark something."

I bite my lip.

"Maybe I need to be closer to the house," I say.

I take a step forward.

Broken concrete crunches under my feet.

Tangled vines scratch my bare ankles.

I take another step.

And another.

Before I get any closer, Sienna screams.

9

I jolt and turn around, heart hammering, expecting ghosts or monsters or murderers.

Instead, a boy about our age with pale skin and fine red hair stands by Sienna's side, his hands raised defensively.

"I'm sorry I'm sorry I'm sorry!" he says on repeat.

I jog over to them.

"You scared me half to death!" Sienna says. "Why'd you sneak up on me like that?"

"I didn't!" he insists. "I saw you from across the street and called out. But you must not have heard me so I came over and, well, you screamed."

Sienna looks to me, eyes wide. "I thought he was a ghost."

"Not a ghost," the boy says. He squeezes the skin on his forearm to prove it. "Just a boy. My name's Mark. Who are you?"

"Sienna," my friend replies.

"Kara," I say.

"What are you *doing* here?" Mark asks. He looks around conspiratorially, then drops his voice. "Don't you know what *happened* in there?"

I glance to Sienna. Her fear quickly turns to excitement.

"Do *you*?" she asks.

Mark regards her, his expression hurt. "'Course I know. Grew up here, didn't I? All the kids in town know the story of Elizabeth Townsend."

He raises an eyebrow.

"But *you're* not from around here. So why are you here?"

I open my mouth, but before I can say something stupid like *I have visions*, Sienna interjects.

"School project," she says haughtily. "We're researching urban legends, and the tale of Elizabeth Townsend came up."

"Oh, she's no urban legend," Mark says. "She's real. Saw her ghost myself."

Chills race over my skin. He's seen her, too?

"You did?" I ask.

Mark nods and points over my shoulder. "Saw her right up there. Was playing outside and looked over. She was up in that window. She just looked at me for a few minutes. Gave me the creeps. Then . . . she just disappeared."

He stares at the house in wonder, then seems to catch himself and hunches up, suddenly defensive.

"And no matter what you say, I know what I saw. She was real. And I don't care if you believe me or not."

"We believe you," I say. "Did you know her? When she was, you know, alive?"

He shakes his head. "She died the same year I was born," he says. "Twelve years ago now."

The same year I was born, too. Does it mean anything?

"Do you know anything else?" I press. "About what happened to her?"

He hesitates.

Now it's Sienna who interjects. "The newspapers say she drowned."

"She did . . ."

There's something in the way Mark says it that tells me he's hiding something.

"What?" I ask. "What is it?"

He looks around. A family on the other side of the street waves at us. He grimaces and waves back. Sienna and I exchange a look. Seriously—why is everyone in town so friendly?

"She wasn't alone when she drowned," he finally says when the family is gone. "She was with her friend."

"James?"

He looks at me strangely. "Yeah. How'd you know about him?"

"Research," I lie. "He'd be, what, twenty-four now?"

"Give or take," he says.

"Maybe we can ask him, then," Sienna says.

"No!" Mark yelps. His eyes are wide and his cheeks flushed. He takes a deep breath to calm himself. "I mean, no. You shouldn't look for him."

"Why not? Having a firsthand account would be super helpful," Sienna says. Then she adds, unconvincingly, "For our report."

Once more, Mark looks around like he's scared, which is strange because it's not like there's anyone *scary* out, unless you count families pushing their infants in strollers.

"Because there's a rumor . . ." He swallows. "A rumor that he wasn't just there. That he pushed her. That he's the reason she drowned."

He'll hurt you, too. That's what Elizabeth said in my visions. Was she talking about James? He hadn't seemed too nice in those diary entries. I might not know him well, but what I read is enough to convince me he'd do something horrible.

"So he killed her?" Sienna asks. "Why isn't he in jail?"

Mark shrugs. "He said it was an accident. A dare gone wrong. He was the one who reported it in the first place."

"So why shouldn't we talk to him, if it was an accident?"

"Because I've never believed it," he finally says. "He's always been a bully. Bad things happen whenever he's around. And . . ." He looks up to the house. "And if it was an accident, why is she still haunting her own house? No. I think James murdered her. And I want to prove it."

10

"**Have you found any leads?**" I ask.

He looks sheepishly down at his feet. "No. James scares me. And so does her ghost."

"So you don't know anything beyond rumors?" Sienna asks.

"I . . . no."

Sienna sighs loudly. I give her a look—it's such a Megan thing to do, I can't believe it's coming from my friend.

"What about her parents?" Sienna asks. "Did you ask them anything?"

"No. They left a few days after Elizabeth's funeral. Never came back." He looks up to the house. "No one's lived here since."

"So it's a dead end," Sienna says bluntly.

"No! I can help," Mark says. "I know this town better than anyone. I bet we can find a lead if we're looking together. Three heads are better than one and all."

"All right, then, where do we start?"

"Well, I gotta do homework. My mom will kill me if I'm not home soon."

"Okay," I reply.

"Are your parents here?" he asks. He says it kindly, but Sienna's eyes narrow.

"Yeah. They're at the hotel downtown. The, what was it called . . . ?"

"Knights Inn?" Mark suggests.

"That's the one!"

"Okay, well. I can swing by in the morning, then. We can explore together."

"I mean . . ." Sienna begins.

"Sure!" I reply. "But why don't we meet here. Ten a.m.? That should be a good time to start exploring."

"Sounds good," he replies. "Have a good night."

With an awkward little wave, he turns and goes. We watch him walk down the street and disappear around the corner.

"Well," I say when he's gone. "What are we going to do?" It feels weird standing in front of the house like this, just the two of us—I've never felt more suspicious in my life, and every smiling family that walks past makes my skin crawl.

"He was our best lead," Sienna replies. "Shame he was such a coward."

She says it so judgmentally I almost gasp. She's never said mean things like that. Unless it was about Megan, who always deserved it.

"What are you talking about?"

"He's lived here his entire life and never did any research. You'd think this James guy is a monster."

"Maybe he is?"

Sienna shrugs. "I feel like the bar for 'monster' is pretty low in a place this disgustingly friendly." She sighs dramatically again. "Well, if we're on our own again, I guess there's only one thing to do."

"Oh?"

"Yup. Time to explore the house!"

She reaches into her backpack and pulls out two big flashlights. She tosses one to me. I almost drop it when trying to catch it. Partly because I'm bad at catching, and partly because the moment she mentioned going inside, I started to shake. And not because of a vision.

Coming here was one thing. But going inside a haunted house? Even if it's the middle of the day, the thought still terrifies me. The only thing that keeps me from turning around and heading back to the bus station is the idea of poor Elizabeth trapped inside.

"Okay," I whisper. "Let's do this before it gets dark." I want to be as far away from here as possible when night falls. Preferably at the hotel Mark mentioned—I hope she managed to book us a room somehow.

We give one last look around to make sure no one is watching—either on the street or from within the house—and then hurry up the front steps. The old wood groans under our feet, but thankfully doesn't give way. The air grows colder with every step and fills with the scent of rot and mildew and dust. It's only been a decade, so why does this place smell and look like it's been abandoned for a century?

"Ready?" Sienna asks.

I'm not. But I nod *yes* anyway.

She pulls the screeching screen door open, then tests the front door. It's unlocked. *Why is it unlocked?*

Together, we slip inside.

The first room is a living room. Or, at least, what's left of one. There are a few sofas and tables scattered about, all of them draped in moth-eaten sheets. Dust is an inch thick on the floor. The windows are boarded up, but little streams of light filter through them, illuminating faded photos on the walls and a big empty fireplace. A staircase leading upstairs is along the wall.

"Whoa," Sienna gasps.

"Creepy," I reply.

"Look at the floor!" she says.

"I know. It's so dusty. I hope you're not allergic."

"No, it's not that. *Nothing* has been here. The dust is undisturbed. Not even mice or spiders or anything."

She's right.

I shine the flashlight around and realize that the dust on every surface is undisturbed. No tracks. No scuffles. Not even a hint of a breeze. No one's been in here.

At least, nothing *alive*.

"Guess ghosts don't leave footprints," Sienna says with a sly grin. Then, before I can say anything, she takes another step into the room, creating a small cloud of dust and leaving a very visible footprint.

No turning back now.

"Should we split up?" she asks.

"No. That's like always the worst idea," I say.

She smiles again. "It's the middle of the day! What could possibly happen?"

"Never say that! Besides, you're the one who screamed when a *living* boy snuck up on you," I remind her. "Imagine how loud you'd be if it was a ghost."

That makes her stop smiling.

"He was creepy. It's not my fault." She gestures toward the next room with her flashlight. "Come on.

If you insist on doing this together, let's keep moving."

We creep from room to room on the main floor. It's not a huge house, not by Midwest standards. There's a living room, and a dining room right next to it, and a kitchen around the corner. Each room is covered in a thick layer of dust. Each has been undisturbed since Elizabeth died. Until we came in.

"Why do you think no one's come in here?" Sienna wonders.

I shrug. "Why would anyone want to?"

"To sell the place? Tear it down? I dunno. Seems like a waste."

"Maybe the ghost scared them away."

She doesn't say anything.

We walk through the kitchen, where a full set of plates and glasses were left in the sink, as if they were just about to be washed after a meal. Thankfully, whatever food was on them is long decayed—there isn't a trace left. On the other wall is a door. Sienna goes up to it and wiggles the doorknob, but it doesn't budge.

"Locked," she says. She gives it a small kick. Dust puffs off the frame. "Probably goes down to the basement. Where they keep the bodies."

"Don't be gross," I reply. I don't want to imagine

that. Also, I don't think there would be any bodies here in the first place, and even if there were, someone would have come in by now and found them. Right? I suddenly wish I didn't read so many scary books—my imagination is going wild.

She laughs and then steps away.

"Come on," she says. "Let's go check out upstairs."

She leaves the kitchen, but I don't follow right away. Something keeps me there. Just for a few moments. I take a step toward the basement door.

And that's when I hear it.

A voice.

Elizabeth's voice.

Calling out my name.

"*Kara,*" the voice calls. "*Kara, you have to leave, please!*"

It's coming from the basement. Her warning sends chills down me, but I can't leave—not when I'm so close.

"Where are you?" I whisper. "How do I get down there?"

"*Please, if he catches you . . . !*"

"Who? Who are you talking about?"

"*Don't be trapped like me!*"

Her final words are a yell, one that rattles the door. I leap back and stumble right into Sienna.

"What is it?" she asks. "Why were you screaming?"

"I wasn't," I say. My whole body is shaking with fear. She wraps me in a hug as I point to the door. "Elizabeth. Down there. She's trapped."

Sienna squeezes me and then walks over to the door. She pushes on it. Shakes the knob. Even peers through the keyhole.

"I don't know how to get in there," she says. "It's too thick to break down."

The diary, I almost tell her. Something holds my tongue. *There has to be a clue in the diary.*

"We'll find a way," I reply.

It's not until we leave the room that I realize I wasn't exactly replying to her.

I was making a promise to Elizabeth.

If we thought the main floor was creepy, the upstairs is even worse.

We nearly slip on the carpeted steps as we walk up—the dust is so thick that it clogs the treads of our shoes and makes the floor as slippery as ice. There are spaces on the wall where photos would have once hung—I have a blurry memory of them from my visions—but it's completely bare. It feels empty but full, like a tomb.

My breath catches when we reach the top step. The stairwell isn't completely devoid of art after all. A large painting hangs before us.

"Is that . . ." Sienna whispers. "Is that her?"

I nod.

She looks exactly as she had in my visions: long brown hair, pale skin, a tight smile.

Exactly as she looked in the photo in the newspaper clipping. Did someone paint this right before she died?

"Guess we're in the right place," Sienna says. She leans forward and taps the picture on the forehead. *"Did James murder you?"* she goads.

I smack her hand away. "Hey, that's not polite."

Sienna shrugs. "Just seeing if it talked. Sometimes they do in the movies, you know. Would save us a lot of trouble."

Without apologizing, she turns and starts walking down the hall.

What's gotten into her? I wonder. She's never this rude. It's almost like she doesn't want to be here and is making me pay for it. But it was her idea to come here in the first place.

Maybe she's just tired, I tell myself. Before she can vanish into another room on her own, I hurry after her.

✗✗✗

The first room we enter must have been Elizabeth's parents' room. The wallpaper is faded and dull, and it contains a big bed with dusty sheets and a wardrobe that holds nothing but moth-eaten clothes. There are a few pictures in here as well—portraits, landscape paintings, and even a giant picture of Elizabeth with her parents standing behind her. They're all smiling, the perfect family. But something about Elizabeth looks . . . off. I lean a little closer.

Even though she's smiling, she doesn't look happy. And it's not like a forced smile from a school photo, when you're more grimacing because you just want it over with. No . . . there's a sadness in her eyes, a heaviness that makes my heart ache.

I'm trapped here, she'd warned. Something in her photo's expression makes me think she felt trapped way before she died.

I grew up in a small town, too. I get it. But at least here, everyone's friendly.

When we turn and leave the room, I swear I feel those sad eyes staring at me.

We check out the other bedroom next. This one is a little smaller than the first, and it's very clearly Elizabeth's. The walls are a faded pink, covered with posters of bands or cartoons. Dolls and stuffed animals are piled atop her bed. Her desk is covered in colored pencils and paper. When I go over and inspect it, I see she had been working on a drawing—a castle in the mountains, with a Pegasus flying over the sun. It's really good. Somehow, even the drawing feels a little sad, even though it's such a happy scene.

"Are you sure no one else has been in here?" Sienna asks. She doesn't step into the room, just stands awkwardly in the doorway. Is she actually scared?

"I don't think so," I say. "Why?"

"No dust," she says simply.

She's right.

Although the curtains are a little faded and worn, and there are a few moth holes in the quilt, there isn't any dust in the room. In fact, it looks like someone was just in here to clean. The bed is tightly made, the floor freshly vacuumed, the dolls and stuffed animals perfectly arranged. Even the tops of the dresser and nightstand are shining in the afternoon light.

"That's too weird," she says. She looks to me, her eyes gleaming with excitement.

Never in my life would I have thought a clean room would creep me out so much.

"It's almost like Elizabeth was getting it ready for you," she says, twisting her voice to make it sound creepy. "Come on, let's see if there are any other surprises here."

The next room is the bathroom, which is just as dusty as everything else. The curtain is covered in holes, and the sink is crusted in limescale and rust. But when Sienna goes over and tests the knob, it works.

"No way," she says as water pours into the sink. "I would've thought they'd have turned the water off by now."

She goes over and flushes the toilet, which works as well. She tests out the bathtub. It takes a moment, but water eventually spills from the faucet.

"It isn't hot," she says. "The water heater probably broke ages ago. But that's fine."

When she turns to me, she's smiling.

"What?" I say. I know that smile. It's the *I have an idea* smile.

"I found our hotel room," she says.

"What? No way. You want us to stay here? What about the Knights Inn?"

"Never heard of it," she says. "Besides, we have everything we need: Food. Toiletries. I even have some spare blankets in the bag."

"You can't mean that," I protest.

"Of course I do. We can't exactly rent a hotel room—we're too young! And unless you want to go ask that weirdo Mark to let us stay in his garage or something . . ."

A part of me wants to be angry. That part suspects that this had been her plan all along. She's always liked creepy things—of *course* she'd want to stay the night in a haunted house. But the rest of me has to admit that she has a point. Save for Elizabeth's bedroom, it's clear that no one has been in here for years. No one would *suspect* anyone of being here, either. It's the perfect hideaway.

But that's not why I agree.

I agree because I *want* to stay here.

I refuse to admit it to her, but no matter how creepy this place is, it feels like home.

12

We spend the rest of the afternoon exploring the old house, looking for secret rooms or a key to the basement. We don't find either. Instead, we find a bunch of photographs in boxes. Most are family trips or reunions, filled with old people whose names are forgotten by time. A few show Elizabeth playing in the front yard with a boy. *James.* I feel a little guilty, but I keep those pictures and hide them in the diary, just in case.

The strangest part is, I don't have any more visions. Sienna keeps asking me if I see or sense anything, but I don't. After the vision this morning, I've had nothing. I don't normally get a bunch in a single day, but I guess I had thought that being here would make them happen. I keep waiting to get a memory of walking down this hall, or staring at this photo. Keep waiting for some ghostly guidance to show up and help us solve this case. It never happens. By the end of the day, we're still no closer to figuring out what happened to Elizabeth, or why I keep being pulled here.

We call it a day when the light in the house grows dim. I can tell I'm not the only one who's disappointed.

"Nothing, huh?" Sienna asks, plopping down in an old armchair. A huge puff of dust billows up around her. She coughs and swats it away. It doesn't help—she's coated in pale white powder.

"Actually . . . maybe!" I say, squinting at her. "I think I see a ghost!"

I point directly at her, and she laughs. It's a forced laugh. We're both tired, and I can tell from her expression that she's trying really hard not to act defeated.

"You look like a ghost yourself," she says.

I look down at my arms, which are coated in dust.

"Who's going to take an ice bath first?" I ask.

She grimaces. "I suppose I can go wipe down at the very least. If I go to sleep like this, I'll be sneezing all night." She doesn't get up to go, however. She bites her lip, looking at everything in the room but me.

"What?" I ask. "What is it?"

"Nothing," she says. She paints on her smile. But I've known her long enough to know when she's upset. And I know why: She was hoping we'd have a clue by now.

She was hoping we wouldn't have to stay the night

in a haunted house. No matter how much she was pretending to be excited earlier, now that it's getting dark and the place is creaking and groaning with our presence, now that home is a hundred miles away and there's no one to come help us if things get scary, it's no longer as enticing. Not even for me. This place is starting to feel less like a home . . . and more like a tomb. I'm suddenly acutely aware of Elizabeth's warning: *Stay away.*

We haven't encountered any real danger here . . . but what if we're about to?

"Tomorrow we should go around town," Sienna says, trying to sound hopeful. "We could check out the lake, and maybe talk to the locals. We only have one full day left before we have to catch the bus home. Maybe if we interview people, we can find out more."

That makes my stomach flip harder than the idea of coming out here in the first place. She wants us to *talk to people*? To *complete strangers*? And sure, Mark was friendly enough, but that doesn't mean everyone will be. If I've learned one thing, it's that adults get really suspicious when unknown kids start asking questions.

I think I'd rather just stay in a haunted house forever.

Before I can worry too much about that, however, someone knocks at the front door.

Both Sienna and I freeze.

We look to the door. There's no way of telling who's out there through the thick wood.

No one knows we're here. Right?

Neither of us moves.

Neither of us dares to breathe.

Silence stretches.

"Should we . . ." Sienna whispers.

BANG

   BANG

 BANG.

The knocking is louder. I fight down a squeak.

Who knows we're here? I want to ask. Did a neighbor or cop see us rooting around in the house? Is it our parents, tracing our phones? Can they even do that?

As my mind races, Sienna bravely stands. She clutches her phone in a quivering hand—I can't tell if she wants to use it to call the authorities or as a weapon.

"Hello?" comes a timid voice from the other side. "Are you still in there?"

I recognize the voice, and my fear dissolves immediately.

"Mark!" I gasp.

Sienna instantly groans.

"What's *he* doing here?" she asks. Then she storms over and yanks open the door.

Mark jumps back when she opens it, nearly dropping the two pizza boxes he was holding.

"You scared me!" he yelps.

"Scared you? You scared *us*!" Sienna says. "Why are you here?"

He holds up the pizza boxes. "I thought you might be hungry," he says.

I get up from the chair and stand beside Sienna.

"What? How did you know we were here?"

"Yeah," Sienna says brusquely. "I thought you believed we were staying at that hotel. The, what was it? Knights Inn?"

Despite his shock from earlier, Mark smiles. "That's kinda how I knew you were staying here."

"How?" Sienna asks.

"There's no such hotel," he says. "I mean, there was. Like, before we were born. But it's a storage place now."

"I—" Sienna opens and closes her mouth, surprised. "I can't believe you did that."

He shrugs. "I didn't want you to think I was being creepy, asking after you. I also wasn't certain you'd be brave enough to stay in a haunted house. Which . . ."

He looks past our shoulders. "Have you seen anything?"

"No," I say.

Sienna glares at me. I ignore her. "Come inside," I continue. "Someone might be watching."

I swear I feel Sienna's glare intensify, but she doesn't refuse as I step out of the way so Mark can come in.

Mark hesitates. "Are you sure it's safe?"

"We've been here all day and haven't found a thing," Sienna says bluntly. She steps aside. "By all means, make yourself at home."

Mark gives me a look, like he's waiting for my permission again. I nod. He steps inside.

"I, um, I like what you did with the place," he says awkwardly.

Sienna doesn't respond. Just grabs a box of pizza and goes to the coffee table in the living room.

"Come on," I tell Mark. And then, quieter, "Don't mind her."

We settle in at the table and start eating. My stomach rumbles happily the moment he opens the boxes—even though we hadn't found anything, we've been moving all day. I'm tired and starving and really want to go home, but the warm cheese pizza makes me feel a little better. It beats the granola bars we packed.

"Thanks for bringing this," I say. Sienna doesn't say another word, just eats her pizza while staring at her phone.

"You're welcome," he says. "So . . . you didn't find any clues? Or glimpses of Elizabeth?"

I shake my head.

"I swear I saw her in the window last week," he says.

"I believe you," I reply. "We were thinking of going into town tomorrow to see if anyone had any leads."

"Good luck with that," he says.

"What do you mean?"

"No one here really likes talking about her death," he says. "It happened over a decade ago, but I think people just prefer to think it never happened."

"Great," I say.

"I might have another option," he says.

This catches Sienna's attention.

"What is it?" she asks.

"I can take you to where she died," he says.

Around us, I swear I hear the house groan.

13

"Everyone knows where she died," Sienna says between mouthfuls of pizza. "It was in the newspaper."

"Well, yeah," Mark says awkwardly. "But, like . . . you haven't been there yet, right?"

I tell him no.

"The lake is huge," he continues. "You'd never find the spot unless you knew where to look."

"And you think, what?" Sienna challenges. "We might find clues there?"

He shrugs. "It can't hurt."

"Tell that to Elizabeth," Sienna mutters under her breath.

I glare at her. I don't know why she's being so mean to Mark when all he's trying to do is be helpful.

"Thanks," I say. "That sounds like a plan. We can check out the lake and then . . . if we don't find anything, we can ask around." I really don't want to talk to people, but I throw that in there to make Sienna feel better. I don't know if it works. She just keeps eating her food.

"Cool," Mark says. "I can meet you back here in the morning?"

"Sure," I reply.

"But if you're late, we're leaving without you," Sienna replies.

"I'll be here by seven, sharp," he says. He looks to me. "If that's okay with you."

Why is everyone looking to me to make the decisions?

"Sure," I say. "That works."

"Great," he replies. "Maybe, if you're there, you'll get a vision."

My heart skips a beat.

Had I mentioned visions?

He must notice my wide eyes. He hurriedly continues, "You know, kinda like what I saw here. Maybe you'll catch a glimpse of what happened to Elizabeth or something."

"Yeah . . ." I say slowly. "Maybe."

He looks at his watch. "Well, I better get home. Don't want my parents wondering where I am." He pauses halfway to standing. "Do *your* parents know where you are? I mean, I know you lied about them staying in town. But they know you're here, right?"

"Of course they do," Sienna says quickly. "In fact, they want us to call soon. So . . . good night."

"Right," he says. "Night."

I accompany him to the door.

"Thanks again for the pizza," I say as I open the door.

"Of course," he says. He looks over my shoulder to Sienna, who is staring at us. "Be careful tonight," he whispers.

"We will," I reply.

"No. Really. This place is dangerous. And Elizabeth . . . well, let's just say she wasn't as innocent as everyone wants you to believe. She had a mean streak. You can't trust her."

"What do you mean?"

"I've had visions of her. And this house. And . . ." He looks at his feet. "Of you. That's how I knew you were here today. I saw it."

"I—"

"I've said too much. Good night."

Before I can say anything else, he darts away.

The moment he's gone, Sienna sighs in relief.

"*Finally,*" she says. "He was really weirding me out."

I'm still reeling over his revelation. *He has visions? Like me?* And, stranger—*he had visions* of *me?* I almost tell her this, but his fear holds my tongue.

Instead, I ask, "Why do you hate him so much?"

"I don't *hate* him," she says. "I just don't trust him. He's being awfully helpful to people he's never met, isn't he?"

That's not entirely true. He's seen me before . . . just not in person.

I want so badly to share his secret, but it isn't mine to tell. "He's just trying to solve the mystery. Like us."

"If you say so," she says. "But I'm not letting my guard down. He's . . . strange."

Her words are a dagger to the heart. Partially because *she's* the one acting strangely, but mostly because Mark is exactly like me. He's just a normal boy plagued with visions about this place, trying to make sense of it all. Trying to make the weird things stop.

Does that mean Sienna thinks I'm strange, too?

Once more, I say nothing.

"I'm going to go rinse off," Sienna says. "If you hear screaming, it's either a ghost, or the water's *really* cold."

"Okay," I say. I know she's trying to be funny, but I can't bring myself to laugh. Her words still sting. And she doesn't even realize it.

When she goes upstairs to the bathroom, I sneak over to the window and peer out the moth-eaten curtain. There's a part of me that wants to call out to him. To ask more about his visions, to learn more about James and the rumors around Elizabeth's death.

But even though I look toward both ends of the street, Mark is already gone.

14

Sienna and I curl up in the bed in Elizabeth's bedroom.

Neither of us comments on how strange it is that the entire room is free of dust, or that the bedsheets smell like they were washed a few days ago. After Sienna's joke earlier, neither of us wants to admit that it truly does feel like the room was prepared just for us.

Neither of us wants to know what that foretells.

We've both rinsed off with washcloths, so I don't feel like I'm coated in dust anymore. But as we settle in, I realize I don't feel clean. Something about this place is seeping into my bones. An unease.

It doesn't matter that I've had visions of Elizabeth for as long as I can remember. Now that we're here, in her house, I don't just feel watched—I feel like I've been lured here. Because it's not just me anymore. Sienna's been dragged into this, too. And, apparently, so was Mark. Why? And why was Elizabeth herself trying to keep me away when she was the one I was constantly having visions of?

We lie on our backs in the dark, watching the streetlight shine on the ceiling. The old house creaks with the night wind, and the cars driving past outside sound like they're a million miles away.

Which makes home feel even farther.

Soon, I hear Sienna's breathing slow as she falls asleep.

Another few minutes pass. I'm not tired at all.

So, as quietly as possible, I slip out of bed and grab my backpack.

I tiptoe down the stairs and settle in on the armchair, trying not to disturb any more dust. I grab a tiny flashlight, open the diary, and start skimming through the pages.

I don't know what I'm looking for, exactly. But my head feels sleepy and my limbs are heavy and as I turn the pages, it almost feels like entering a trance.

Then I pause on an entry.

Sept 15

I have to get out of here.
I've known it forrever. But no one else seems to understand.

When I told my parents I wanted to leave, they looked at me like I had cursed at them. Mom wanted to ground me, but Dad told her not to. Instead, they said that it was dangerus outside. That other people couldn't be trusted.

I asked if we could just go on a small trip. To a zoo maybe. Or an adventure park.

No.

I told James. I don't know why. He made fun of me. He said only stupid people try to leave town.

Am I stupid? Is something wrong with me?

Sept 17

James says I need to be distracted. He says I'll stop thinking of leaving once I realize how grate this place is.

He thinks we should start pranking people.

I don't like the idea. But James bullied me into it.

So we played a prank. On Mr. Pierce. I don't know why. James just doesn't like him. We eggd his house.

I think James broke a window, but I'm not sure.

I just hope Mr. Pierce didn't see us. We did it at night. So we could hide in the dark. When we walked past this morning his house was all covered in gross eggs. It smelled really bad.

I didn't see Mr. Pierce, but I heard him inside. I think he was crying.

James laffed. I laffed, too. But I felt bad.

I still feel bad.

I want to tell Mr. Pierce the truth. But James scares me.

Now I really want to leave.

I pause when I'm done reading. Mark said that Elizabeth wasn't entirely innocent—is that what he meant? But egging a house isn't exactly an excuse for murder.

The house creaks. Lights flicker along the wall. A car?

But I didn't hear one drive past.

"Stop freaking yourself out," I whisper.

I skip a few pages and keep reading.

Oct 2

Mr. Pierce is so mad. He stands outside all day and all night, waiting for kids to come by so he can yell at them. James and I stand on the corner and watch from the bushes. Today, Mr. Pierce screamed at a little kid who was riding her bike. The kid cried. Mr. Pierce laffed.

James says we should teach him a lesson. Again.

I don't know.

Mr. Pierce scares me.

Oct 20

It's almost Halloween. My favoritt holiday. But I'm not in the spirit (hah, get it?). James wants to pull the prank Halloween night.

He won't tell me what it is. He says it will make Mr. Pierce nice to us once and for all.

I don't know if anything will ever make that grump nice. But James is my only friend. And I don't like feeling scared of Mr. Pierce.

Nov 1

We did it.
We sholdn't have. But we did it.

My breath is stuck in my throat. What did they do? But the next few pages are ripped out. If Elizabeth wrote down her prank, she or someone else removed the evidence. I'm about to close the diary—my eyes are getting tired—when the words on the next page catch my attention. There are only a few pages left, after the rest that were ripped out.

Feb 3

He's following me.
He's always following me.

Feb 4

I saw him outside my window last night.
On the sidewalk. Looking up.
Why won't he leave me alone?

Feb 7

I don't want to go outside.
If I go outside, he'll get me.
He might get me inside, too.

"I told you to stay away."
The words jolt me. A girl's voice. At first I think it's Sienna, then I realize it isn't coming from upstairs.

It's coming from the kitchen.

I turn, my skin freezing like ice, to see Elizabeth

floating

in front

of me.

It takes me a moment to realize what's happening.

I'm not having a vision. My sight isn't tilting. The world isn't going gray.

I'm sitting on the armchair in the real world, in real time, and Elizabeth is really in front of me.

At least, the ghost of her is.

She floats in the middle of the doorway, her toes just inches from the ground. Her eyes are sad, and her hair and clothing float around her like she's underwater.

"Elizabeth," I gasp.

I blink and she's floating right in front of the couch. Her eyes are level with mine. There's nothing happy within them. Her eyes are shadowed with black. Her irises pull me down, down, like hollow pits sucking all life from my veins.

"I told you not to come here," she says. And there isn't just sadness in her voice—there's anger.

I suppress a shudder.

I never thought about what might happen if Elizabeth didn't want me to find her.

She isn't as innocent as they want you to think.

"I came here to help you," I say. "To set you free."

"You can't set me free," she says. Again, the sadness mixed with rage.

"Who did this to you? How did you die? Why are you trapped here?" So many questions burn through my skull, but I can't manage to ask the one I really want answered: *Why have you been cursing me with visions my entire life?*

"You need to leave," she says. She turns. Begins to float away. "Before it's too late."

"But I—"

"NOW!" Elizabeth's scream makes the whole house rattle. Dust billows up around her, a mini sandstorm, and when I blink away the tears, I see her face in the whirlwind. It's no longer the girl I know: This is a face of fury and frustration, of rage and regret. Her skin is cracked, her eyes black holes, her lips slashes of black.

The wind lashes at me, making me stumble off the chair. I try to cover my eyes with my hands as the diary falls to the ground.

Instantly, the wind dies down. To reveal Elizabeth, floating before me, confusion clear on her face as she looks down at the diary.

"My diary," she whispers. "Where did you get that? How?"

"It was sent to me," I say.

"But who—"

"Who is that?" Sienna calls from upstairs.

I look back. She stands at the top of the steps, holding a flashlight.

Her beam illuminates the floating dust. But Elizabeth is gone.

"Nothing," I say. "It was nothing."

15

I wake up, except I know I'm not awake, because the living room isn't dusty and Sienna is nowhere in sight. Sun beams through the windows, illuminating a living room filled with fresh flowers and smiling photographs and furniture that looks brand-new.

Another vision.

A moment later, Elizabeth comes running down the stairs, tears pouring down her cheeks.

She rushes toward me, clutching something to her chest—and then runs *through* me as she races toward the kitchen.

I don't feel a thing, not even a gust of wind.

I hurry after her.

She runs past her mom, who calls out, "What's wrong, sweetie?" but Elizabeth doesn't stop. She opens the basement door and runs downstairs. I'm right behind her.

Elizabeth goes straight toward the brick wall. Quickly, crying, she pulls out a loose brick and shoves something behind it. I try to move around her to get a better look, but she's too fast. She slides the brick back into place and leans against the wall, breathing heavily.

A loud KNOCK upstairs makes her startle and look up to the ceiling. Her eyes go wide as a rabbit's.

A few seconds later, her mom calls out, "Elizabeth, you have a visitor!"

Elizabeth swallows. Tries to plaster on a fake smile.

"Coming, Mom!" she says back.

She takes a step away from the wall. Looks back at the brick she'd displaced.

"At least now he can't hide from the truth."

When she turns back, she looks straight at me.

"But if he finds out you know . . . you'll never leave here. Just like I can't."

16

"How'd you sleep?" Mark asks bright and early the next day. He stands at the back door—I guess he didn't want to alert the neighbors that we were here, now that it's daylight—with a big grin on his face.

"Not good," I reply. I stifle a yawn. It feels like I didn't sleep at all.

"Bad dreams?"

I glance to Sienna. She's by the sofa, repacking her bag. I haven't told her about what happened last night—about seeing Elizabeth, and also about the weird dream. I know it's strange, but I almost feel more comfortable telling Mark about it than her. Even though she's my best friend, she's gotten so . . . judgmental.

"You could say that," I reply simply.

Mark nods. "Makes sense. A place like this is bound to give you bad dreams. Did you—"

I can tell he's about to ask if I've seen Elizabeth, but before he can, Sienna claps me on the shoulder.

"We gonna go, or stand around here wasting time?"

"Let's go!" Mark says without missing a beat. "I was thinking we could grab breakfast on our way to the lake." He eyes the granola bar Sienna's holding. "Unless you're okay with that?"

"Perfectly fine, thanks," she says.

"Actually," I say, "that would be great."

Sienna glares at me. Mark grins—I can't tell if it's because I agreed with him, or if it's because he likes seeing Sienna upset. He doesn't seem like that sort of person, though.

"Let's go, then," he says.

We take off, and maybe it's my imagination, but it seems like there are a lot more people out and about. Everyone we pass smiles and waves and makes eye contact, especially when they see we're with Mark.

"Hi, Mark!" a mom calls out from across the street. Her two kids wave. He waves back.

"Do you know her?" Sienna asks.

"Of course!" he replies, like Sienna's silly for asking. "I know everyone here." He pauses, looking between the two of us. "Isn't it like that where you're from?"

"Not even close," Sienna says. "Mom always told me not to talk to strangers."

"Everyone's a stranger until you've met them," Mark says. "I mean, I was a stranger to you both yesterday."

"Yeah, but you're not a serial killer or kidnapper or anything," I say.

"True," he says. "But . . . well, nothing bad happens here. We aren't scared of each other."

"What about James?" Sienna asks. "If you suspect him of murdering Elizabeth, shouldn't you be scared of him?"

Mark hesitates. "Yeah," he admits. "But he's just one guy. I know to avoid him."

"What does he look like?" Sienna presses. "So *we* can avoid him. Or interrogate him."

"Sienna!" I gasp.

"What?" she replies. "I'm only kidding. I wouldn't be caught alone in a room with a killer."

But I can tell she's not entirely kidding.

"Well," Mark says, "he's tall. White. Thin. Straight black hair. I dunno, he looks like any other twenty-four-year-old."

"Super helpful," Sienna says.

"I'll point him out if we see him," Mark says. "From a distance."

But we don't see him. Mark leads us to a bakery a block from the school. It seems to take forever to get there. Everyone we pass waves or says hello or asks how Mark or his parents are doing. A few ask about us, but most just eye Sienna and me with a friendly sort of curiosity. Until we get to the café.

"Hello, Mark!" says the owner, a middle-aged Chinese man who quickly introduces himself as Craig. "How are you this morning? And who are your friends?"

Sienna strides over and holds out her hand. "I'm Cheyenne," she says. "And this is my friend Gertrude."

I swallow my gut reaction. Since when do we have code names? Sienna casts a quick glare at Mark, demanding he not say anything. Mark just plasters on a grin.

"Nice to meet you both," Craig says. "You two aren't from around here, are ya?"

Sienna shakes her head. "No, we're from out of town. We're here doing research for a school project."

"Oh? Can't imagine there's too much interesting going on here."

"Well, maybe not anymore. But we're researching Elizabeth Townsend's death."

There's a pause. A brief, tense moment when Craig looks to Mark. I don't know what that look is trying to convey, but it sends chills down my spine.

A moment later, Craig gives a sad smile.

"A tragic story," he says. "She was such a sweet girl. Though this is why we advise against swimming in the lake on your own. It may look peaceful, but there are spots where even strong swimmers can go down."

"I heard she wasn't alone," Sienna says. "I heard she was with her friend, James. Do you know him?"

Again, that look. Again, the chills across my skin.

"James? Why, yes. Though we don't see much of him anymore. Keeps to himself nowadays."

"Do you think he did it?" Sienna asks.

"Did what?"

"Kill her?"

To my surprise, Craig laughs. "Kill her? No way! Not our James. He was a sweet boy—still is! No, they were good friends. He wouldn't have hurt her. He wouldn't have hurt a fly."

"Thanks, Craig," Mark says. "That's helpful for their report. But we were actually here for some breakfast before exploring the town."

"Of course! What can I get you? On the house, of course."

"What?" I ask. "No, we can pay." I've never liked people paying for me.

"Don't be silly. Intrepid investigators need their fuel! It's the least I can do. Though don't spend all day looking into the past. You'll miss just how incredible this place is!"

We order our food, and Craig refuses to let us pay (though I slip some money into the tip jar when his back is turned). When we leave and round the corner, Mark turns to Sienna.

"What was that all about?" he asks.

"What?"

"Questioning Craig. That wasn't nice. I told you that people don't like talking about what happened."

"Yeah, but we aren't going to learn anything if we don't at least try." She takes a bite of her breakfast sandwich. "Maybe we should try to find James. I bet I can crack him."

"No!" Mark yells. He takes a deep breath and calms himself. "I mean . . . no. It wouldn't be safe."

"I can take care of myself," Sienna says.

"I never said you couldn't. But James was different. Everyone here is friendly. But not him. Not really. He and Elizabeth were kind of the rebels." He looks between Sienna and me. His eyes are grave. "Just stay away from him. Please. If he knew you were looking into Elizabeth's death, well . . ." He looks down to his feet. "Well, he might not want you to find out the truth. And he might do whatever he could to stop you."

17

"Over there's the elementary school," Mark says, pointing down a street. "And the middle school is a few blocks that way. The high school is actually pretty close to the lake. Only a few more blocks."

Sienna gives me a look as she chews her sandwich. One that very clearly says *we didn't come here to get a full tour of the town*. But thankfully, she's too busy eating to say it.

It's then that a thought crosses my mind: I still haven't asked Mark about Mr. Pierce. With everything else going on, it had completely slipped my mind. I mean, he made it sound like James was the main suspect. But what about Mr. Pierce? If Elizabeth and James pulled a prank on him, maybe Mr. Pierce wanted revenge?

"Mark," I begin. "You know everyone in town, right?"

Mark nods. "Of course."

"So do you know someone named Mr. Pierce?"

"Yeah," he says.

"Do you think that he might be the cause of Elizabeth's death?"

"Doubtful. And it wouldn't matter even if he was."

"What do you mean?" Sienna asks.

"Because Mr. Pierce died last year," he replies. "Besides, he was really old when Elizabeth died. He couldn't have hurt a fly, even if he wanted to."

It makes me think of what I read in Elizabeth's diary. *She* sure seemed to think that Mr. Pierce was capable of hurting people.

"Where'd you hear the name, anyway?" Mark asks.

"Research," I reply. "I think they interviewed him in one of the papers."

"Right," he replies. "Well, too bad it's a dead end."

"Emphasis on *dead*," Sienna mutters. I nudge her, and she just looks at me. "What?"

I don't say anything.

xXx

A few minutes later, we reach the lake.

It's just like I saw in my dream. Not that there's really a big difference in how lakes look. It's not that big—maybe the size of three football fields—and a walking path curves all the way around it. Willow and maple trees lean over the banks, and ducks circle lazily beneath the branches. Even though it's early, a few people are already walking the loop.

"Over here," Mark says, gesturing.

We follow him over to a place beside a willow. Lily pads float on the murky surface, and frogs tan themselves in the shallows.

"This is where they found her," Mark says quietly.

We stare at the water for a few silent moments before Sienna speaks.

"Okay, so—what happened to her? If the news reports say she drowned, why are you convinced it was her friend?" She looks to Mark when she asks the last part. Her gaze is suspicious—it's then I remember she doesn't know that he's had visions, too. Maybe he saw her drown?

He shrugs.

"I looked into the reports," he said. "It just didn't add up. I . . . don't want to go into the details, but it didn't really look like she drowned. And they found evidence of James at the scene. He had been there, but he hadn't told anyone about it."

"Then why didn't anyone investigate?"

"Like I said, this town wants to forget it ever happened," Mark says. "Easier to blame it on a silly mistake than a murder."

"Have you ever told anyone your suspicions?" Sienna asks.

"No," he replies. "I mean, I tried. But no one listened. Who's going to believe a kid?"

He sounds sad when he says it. I reach out and pat him on the shoulder.

"It's okay, we believe you. We're listening."

He smiles faintly. "Thanks." He takes a deep breath, clearing the air. "Did you want to walk around the lake?"

Sienna looks to the other shore, where a kid is currently popping wheelies on his bike.

"Nah," she replies. "I've seen water before."

Mark chuckles. "Kara?" he asks.

I consider. I was hoping that I'd get a vision now that I'm here, but just like in the house, Elizabeth is being oddly silent. And it's not like we're going to find any clues in the water, over a decade after her death.

"We can go," I say. "Guess there really isn't much here to see."

"Okay then, I'll take you back to town."

He turns and walks away, Sienna close at his side. I stand there a little while longer, looking out over the water, wondering what happened to the girl who is haunting me. I run over everything we've learned: James was her friend, but he is also a suspect. He had dragged Elizabeth into some pretty nasty pranks, including some against a man named Mr. Pierce. But

Mr. Pierce is gone, so I can't question him. That just leaves James.

"Are you coming?" Mark asks.

"Yeah," I say. "Sorry."

I take a step after them . . .

and someone grabs my wrist from behind.

My vision tilts as I turn around, to see Elizabeth standing in the shallows. Her expression is terrified.

"He wants you!" she says. *"You have to hurry. You have to leave here!"*

We can't leave! I think in return. *Not until we know what happened to you!*

"You have to. If he gets you—"

"Hey, you coming?" Mark asks.

I jolt back to reality to see him and Sienna staring at me. I look around. Elizabeth isn't there.

"Sorry," I reply. "I thought I heard something."

They both give me questioning looks, but neither presses it. I hurry after them, my heart hammering in my chest. Who is after us? James? Mr. Pierce? The last should sound stupid—Mr. Pierce is dead—but if Elizabeth can haunt me, maybe Mr. Pierce can, too.

It's only when I'm a few steps from the water's edge that I realize my wrist where Elizabeth grabbed me is wet.

18

We reach the downtown area a little while later. It's nearly noon, and the area is filled with families or solo walkers grabbing coffee or lunch. Once more, every person who sees us waves and smiles. Even though it's friendly, it makes me feel strange. Back home, I could mostly walk around without anyone paying attention to me. Here, I feel like I'm on display. I don't like it.

"Are you sure you want to do this?" I ask Sienna. "Maybe we could just, you know, go to the library or something."

"I'm positive," Sienna says. She puts on a winning smile. "Besides, who *wouldn't* want to talk to me?"

Without waiting for an answer, she heads over to the nearest couple, not even bothering to see if we follow. I look to Mark.

"I'm sorry," I mutter. "She's not normally like this."

"It's fine," he says. He lowers his voice as he looks over to Sienna, who is talking happily with her first victims. "Did you see anything last night? Did you see her?"

I open my mouth to tell him about the weird dream. Before I can, Sienna's words from last night float through my head: *I don't trust him.* I look at Mark for a moment. He seems kind and honest, and he's been nothing but helpful so far. But Sienna's words are like a poison in my brain—I can't get them out, and they taint everything.

"No," I say. "I didn't see her."

"Oh," he says, clearly disappointed. "I thought, when you said you didn't sleep well . . ."

I force a grin. "That's just because I was sleeping in an armchair. Come on, let's go help Sienna."

I start to walk, but Mark holds back.

"Aren't you coming?" I ask.

He looks over my shoulder to the guy Sienna was talking to. He's now walking—quickly—away from her.

"I'll wait over there in the park for you," he says, pointing to a small park a block away. "It's probably best if I'm not asking questions."

"Why?"

He shrugs. "Like I said. People here don't like talking about Elizabeth's death. They remember. And, well, you two get to leave when this is all over. I have to stay and live with their stares."

"Ah. Okay. Well, um. Hopefully this won't take too long."

"Take your time," he says.

I walk over to Sienna, who quickly pulls me into their conversation.

"And this is my friend Gertrude. She's the one spearheading the report."

"Nice to meet you," the woman says.

"Welcome to town," says the man.

"We're so happy you're here," the woman continues. The man gives her a look, and she quickly says, "We don't get many visitors in town. Especially not youngsters like yourselves. It's nice to see a bit of youthful energy."

Sienna smiles awkwardly, and I feel myself cringe. Are these people real? Who says *youngsters* anymore?

"Thanks, I guess," Sienna says. "We knew we had to visit to learn more for our school report."

"Oh!" says the man. "What's it on?"

"Elizabeth Townsend," I reply.

If I wasn't watching them so closely, I would have missed the slight pause, the flicker in their expressions that says they know something but don't want to talk about it.

But they cover, and the man quickly says, "Poor

Elizabeth. What happened to her was such a tragedy."

"And it's why we are now extra careful about ensuring our kids don't go to the lake unsupervised," says the woman.

"I heard it wasn't an accident," Sienna says. "I heard that someone drowned her. We have a small list of suspects. Do you know anyone named James? He'd be in his twenties by now?"

"James? Why would you suspect him? He was her best friend."

"Yes, but—"

"No, James would never do anything to her. In fact, no one would do anything to hurt anyone in our town. We don't have any crime. Save for that one accident, nothing bad has ever happened here. Why don't you write your report on that?"

I want to give in, but Sienna presses on.

"Are you sure? She didn't ever upset anyone? Hurt anyone who would want to hurt her? Say, a neighbor? Mr. Pierce?"

"Elizabeth was an angel," the woman says. "No one would want to hurt her. No one would want to hurt anybody."

"I know . . ." Sienna says slowly. "You already told us that."

"Yes, well, it bears repeating," the man says. "I think a report on Elizabeth is terribly sad. You should write about something more uplifting. Like how—"

"There's no crime here?" Sienna asks. She looks at me, then back to the couple. "Maybe you're right. Well, thank you for that idea. We should keep interviewing people."

"What's the rush?" says the man. "Take your time. Stay awhile. Everyone here is friendly. I'm sure you'll get all the answers you need."

"Thanks," I say.

As we walk away, I realize we never got their names.

"That was weird," Sienna says when we're out of earshot.

"Yeah," I reply. "It's like they were reading from a script."

Sienna looks around. "You know, I'm starting to not like this place."

"Are you saying you want to leave?"

"No. I'm just saying we need to keep our guards up. Come on, let's go ask someone else."

×✗✗

We approach at least twenty different people throughout the afternoon, and every time it goes exactly the same: They are friendly. Overly polite. They tell us how amazing the town is and how nothing bad could ever happen there. And they completely clam up when it comes to Elizabeth Townsend. They all say it was an accident. They all stress that it couldn't have been foul play, that no one in this town would do something like that. Then they say we should go check out a park or local history museum or something else, and that maybe if we stuck around we'd see just how great this place was and just how impossible it would be for bad things to happen.

It seriously feels like being stuck in some weird looping dialogue. One where everyone in the town is in on it.

Except for Mark.

"How'd it go?" he asks when we approach him.

"Not great," I admit.

"Yeah, what's with everyone?" Sienna asks. "Is this town like a cult or something? I swear everyone is way too happy."

Mark grimaces. "Try living here. I told you you wouldn't learn anything."

"We've learned just how great the town is," Sienna says.

"And how nothing bad could ever happen here," I continue.

"Are you *sure* you can't point out James?" Sienna asks. We approached a few different guys around his age while interviewing, but it was never him.

"No," Mark says firmly. "And if you knew better, you'd stay away from him, too."

"Fine, fine," Sienna says. "Just asking."

"It's okay," Mark says. His face brightens. "Want to go to lunch? There's a really good diner down the street."

"Um . . . sure," I say. At least it means not talking to people anymore. My social battery is completely drained.

Mark leads the way, and we soon find ourselves in a normal-looking diner that smells like greasy fries and old coffee. My stomach rumbles. Even though we ate a few hours ago, all that talking to strangers has me starving.

Unfortunately, it doesn't look like that talking is going to stop anytime soon.

"Hey, Mark!" the waitress says when we sit down. "Who are your new friends?"

"Kara and Sienna," Mark says. "They're visiting."

"So I see! It's nice to see new kids in town. What brings you here?"

"Just a weekend trip," I quickly say. Sienna glares at me. But I don't care—the last thing I want right now is to talk to another adult about how great this town is, when all we want to know is what happened to Elizabeth.

The waitress looks to Mark, then back to us.

"Where are you staying?" she asks.

"Our parents got us a hotel in the town nearby," Sienna says. Clearly, she learned her lesson after Mark. "I can't remember what it's called, though."

"Oh, you don't want to stay there!" the waitress says. "You should stay at my cousin's place. She's got a nice little B and B a few blocks away. Here, why don't I give you her card?"

She roots around in her pocket before we can say yes or no, then hands the card over.

"You'll love it," she says. "In fact, I bet she'll even give you a discount if you mention I told you about it. Third night's free."

"Thanks, but we're actually leaving tomorrow."

"Oh! Now why would you do that? Leaving so soon."

"School?" Sienna asks.

The waitress smiles and winks conspiratorially. "I'm sure they won't mind if you miss a few days. We've all played hooky now and again."

"I . . . um . . ." I mutter. I feel my cheeks flush, and I'm really wishing we had just gotten another sandwich to go.

Thankfully, we're saved from further awkward conversation by another customer coming in.

"I better go," the waitress says. "I'll be back to take your order shortly. And Mark, you tell these girls just how great it would be if they stayed just a bit longer. You know Ethel's B and B is worth it!"

"That was a lot," Sienna says when the waitress is gone.

Mark doesn't say anything at first. When he does, it's hesitant.

"She can be a bit much," he admits. "But she raises a good point."

"What do you mean?" I ask.

"You're not going to find much by tomorrow. So, like, maybe you *should* stay a few extra days?"

"Are you kidding? Our parents would kill us!" Sienna says.

"I thought they knew you were here?"

Sienna's eyes widen.

"They do. But they would never let us miss school," I cover. "And they wouldn't pay for a B and B."

"I can talk to her if you want. Maybe she'd do a friends-and-family discount. Let you stay for free."

"Did you not hear the part about missing school?" Sienna asks.

He throws up his hands. "I'm not saying you have

to! Just that it might be an option if you don't learn anything about Elizabeth's death. I'd hate for you to go back empty-handed, and it would be safer than staying in her place."

"Not a chance," Sienna says.

"Okay," Mark says. "Okay."

The waitress comes back over. Thankfully, she only takes our order. But when the food comes around, I realize all this talk has killed my appetite. The more I hear about how great this place is, the more I feel like I need to leave.

As soon as possible.

19

We decide to check out the library after. Mark says he needs to go home and do some chores, but he offers to swing by in a few hours to get us. We agree, and he walks us to the library.

"Think we'll find anything here?" Sienna asks.

"Can't hurt," I reply. "Maybe the local paper has some hints. Or we could try to find out more about Mr. Pierce, or James."

"Let's just hope no one tries to rope us into buying real estate," Sienna says.

"I know, right? It's weird."

"*Very* weird. The sooner we learn who killed Elizabeth, the better. This town is starting to give me the creeps."

At least inside the library everything seems, well, *normal*. The librarian is about my dad's age, wearing a button-down shirt printed with penguins, and has short choppy hair that's dyed blue at the tips. He's probably the coolest-looking librarian I've ever seen.

He looks up at our entrance and smiles warmly.

"Hello," he says. "Haven't seen you two around here before."

My guard instantly goes up, as does Sienna's. Thankfully, he doesn't start regaling us with how amazing the town is. Instead, he holds out his hand. "I'm Mr. Hughes, the librarian. But please, call me Kevin."

I exchange a look with Sienna, then go forward to take his hand.

I shake his hand. "Nice to meet you."

"You must be Kara," he says to me. Then he looks to Sienna. "And Sienna."

My heart flips. "How did you know?"

"Your friend Mark was just mentioning you. I'm friends with his parents. He said you're here researching something for school . . . though he conveniently left out *what* you're researching."

Even though he's friendly, I'm suddenly grateful I live in a bigger town. I can't imagine living in a place where everyone knows everything about you, all the time.

"Yeah, well, people haven't really been all that helpful," Sienna says. "That's why we came here."

"Well then, let's hear it," Mr. Hughes says. "I just moved here a few years ago, but I can probably help point you in the direction of any experts if I don't know." He gestures to the shelves. "This place is filled with the greatest minds in history. And mine, too."

"Well," Sienna says, glancing at me. Here we go. "We were looking into a local urban legend."

"A *real* legend," I interject. "About a real girl."

Mr. Hughes's eyes immediately narrow. He looks around. We're the only ones in the library, but he's still on guard.

"You mean Elizabeth Townsend?"

"Yes!" Sienna exclaims. "What do you know about her?"

Mr. Hughes looks around once more.

"Not much," he says. "Only what I've read in the paper. People here don't like to talk about it."

"So we've noticed," Sienna mumbles.

"Why is that?" I ask. "It happened over a decade ago, but people act like they're still trying to hide from it."

"That's not what they're trying to hide from," Mr. Hughes says gravely.

"What? The killer? But Mr. Pierce is dead." Sienna's words feel too loud in the library. Even *she* winces.

"No one knows for sure that it was him," Mr. Hughes says. "He was the prime suspect but was never charged. If you've come here, you know what the papers say—Elizabeth drowned in the lake. An accident. But Mr. Pierce still got the blame." He shakes his head. "He was never the same after that. Before, locals would see him in town. He was never friendly, but he came in to get his groceries or grab a coffee at the diner. After Elizabeth's death, however, he changed."

"How?" I whisper.

Mr. Hughes shrugs. "Again, all I have are stories, and scant ones at best. But apparently, he locked himself away in his house. Boarded up his windows and doors. Got all his groceries delivered through a doggie door on the front stoop. No one ever really saw him again. Not until . . ."

"He died," Sienna completes.

Mr. Hughes nods. "Everyone thought that was the end of things. That life could go back to normal. But they were wrong."

"What do you mean?" I whisper.

"After Mr. Pierce died," Mr. Hughes replies, just as quietly, "people started complaining about a 'presence.' Something mean. Something evil. It was just rumors at first, stories overheard at the café or in the store. But soon the stories started to gain traction. People were seeing things at night. Shadows with burning eyes that followed them home. And whatever that presence was, it only followed those who talked about Elizabeth Townsend."

His words settle into the library like dust. I shiver.

"Eventually, people stopped talking about Elizabeth and what happened altogether. Her parents left town. The house was abandoned, never to be sold. And everyone tried their best to forget. It seemed like the only way to keep themselves safe. As far as I know, no one's seen or felt that evil presence since." He shrugs. "So maybe it's working."

"Guess that explains why no one wants to talk about her," Sienna says. "Self-preservation."

"Have *you* ever sensed it?" I ask Mr. Hughes.

He shakes his head. "Never. Like I said, I moved here a few years ago. Long after Elizabeth and Mr. Pierce and the fairy stories. I only knew about it from an old paper I read. I did a little digging but never turned up much. The most that people would say was that they wouldn't say anything."

He grins a little. "This is the most I've ever talked about it," he admits. "So if I get haunted tonight, I'm blaming you."

My throat constricts at the thought.

"We'll get to the bottom of it before anything happens," Sienna says. She pauses. "Which . . . do you have any idea of where to look?"

"There's nothing in the library, I'm afraid," he replies. "So, short of investigating Mr. Pierce's or Elizabeth's houses yourselves, I think you may have hit a dead end. Some stories are meant to stay buried."

I know precisely where we need to go next. I share a look with Sienna. Mr. Hughes catches it.

"Now, you most definitely should *not* go investigate those houses. It's dangerous. And illegal, too."

"Don't worry, Mr. Hughes," Sienna says, plastering on her sweet, innocent smile. "We wouldn't dream of it."

20

Fifteen minutes later, we stand outside Mr. Pierce's house.

If we thought that Elizabeth's home was scary, this is pure nightmare.

It's a tall, creaking structure, the yard filled with scraggly dead trees that claw at the blue sky with blackened limbs. Thornbushes tangle both sides of the front steps, which are wooden and broken like splintered bones. The house itself is a faded, cracked white, moss and soot staining it like a corpse. Mr. Hughes wasn't exaggerating, either—every single window is boarded up, making the whole thing look like a prison for some type of terror.

"You're sure it's safe to go in there?" I ask Mark. He was waiting for us the moment we left the library— apparently his chores hadn't taken too long.

"Positive. I've been in there loads of times."

"You have?" Sienna asks suspiciously.

"Well, no. Once. But it was fine! It looks a lot worse on the outside, promise. Come on."

He hurries toward the side of the house. Sienna pauses.

"You're sure we trust him?" she asks.

"Yes," I say. *He has visions like me. That* has *to mean something!* "Besides, it's not like we have any other leads."

"But what are we expecting to find in there? A note admitting Mr. Pierce did it?"

"I don't know. What were *you* expecting to find coming to this town?"

Her eyes widen. I've never spoken back to her like that before. But I'm tired from not sleeping well, and the lack of answers has me on edge. I thought this would be easy. I thought we could just show up and immediately solve Elizabeth's murder. I couldn't have been more wrong.

"Answers," she says. Suddenly, a sad look crosses her face. "And to get my friend back."

Her words are a spear to my heart, punching the air from my lungs.

"What are you talking about?" I ask.

She bites her lip as she considers her words, glancing over to Mark, who's just reached the porch. "The last few weeks, you've gotten . . . Look, it doesn't matter. Let's just get this over with."

She starts walking away before I can ask her what she means. I stand there for a few moments. Did she mean all the visions I was having? I didn't think I was acting any different, but . . .

"You coming?" Mark calls.

I jolt and start walking forward. I make it two steps before my vision shifts.

"Don't."

The world tilts as I'm overcome with a vision.

Elizabeth's ghost floats on the broken path before me; I can see the boarded-up front door and Mark and Sienna through her transparent body.

Elizabeth's dark eyes are pleading.

"Don't go in there," she begs.

"Why not?" I ask.

Her lip trembles.

"You have to leave. You have to leave now!"

"I—"

"Kara, you coming?"

Sienna's voice snaps me from the vision. I reel slightly, pressing a hand to my forehead. The world spins and wobbles around me. But when I manage to take a few deep breaths and blink it away, Elizabeth and all traces of the vision are gone.

"Are you okay?" Sienna asks. She doesn't ask if I've had a vision, not with Mark right there.

"Yeah," I say. "Fine."

I make my way toward them, doing my best not to wobble as I walk. It's not entirely from the aftereffects of the vision, either—Elizabeth's words have chilled my veins. Why does she want us to leave?

I push the questions and the doubt aside and continue on. Once we learn what happened to her, we can go home. And this will all be over.

"How do we get in?" I ask when I reach them. The door is completely boarded up, as are all the windows.

"Through here," Mark says. He gestures over to a window. Then, looking around to make sure no one is watching, he rotates a board up. It had been dangling by a single nail, revealing a space just large enough for us to squeeze through. "After you," he says.

"No," Sienna replies. "After you."

He shrugs and ducks inside, the board swinging shut after him.

"Do we really want to do this?" I ask.

"This was your idea in the first place," Sienna responds.

"I know, but . . ."

"Too late to back out now," she says. And before either of us can chicken out, she lifts the board and sneaks inside.

I follow. I swear, right before I duck through, that I hear Elizabeth calling out to me, telling me to run.

When the board swings shut behind me, I am encased in blackness.

21

Light flares a few moments later when Mark turns on a flashlight. He tosses one to Sienna and one to me. We quickly turn them on and scan the room.

Unlike Elizabeth's house, Mr. Pierce's home isn't even remotely welcoming.

Every piece of furniture has been smashed to pieces and strewn about the scratched wooden floor. Holes gape through walls, revealing more destroyed rooms farther in. There are even great holes in the floorboards, as if meteors had crashed through here. Mice droppings litter the corners, amid chewed-up food cartons and tattered clothes.

"I thought you said it was nicer inside," Sienna says, looking around in disgust.

"Watch your step" is all Mark says in response.

"Don't have to tell me twice," Sienna says. "Where do we go first? And don't you dare suggest we split up."

Mark chuckles. "Of course not. It's best we stay in a group. Where did you want to go?"

Sienna considers. "Let's check out the basement."

"You sure? There's nothing down there," Mark says.

"And it's going to be dark," I reply, my voice shaking.

"Wouldn't you rather inspect the darkest room in the house while it's still bright out?" Sienna challenges.

I open my mouth to argue, then close it.

"I guess you have a point," I admit.

Sienna looks to Mark. "Well? Lead on."

Mark nods and moves farther into the house, ducking past a dismantled sofa. Sienna follows.

I take a step.

My vision shifts once more.

"DON'T!"

Elizabeth's voice is so loud, the vision so physical, that I stagger back against the wall, nearly tripping over a board in the process.

It's over immediately, but it still makes my head throb. A second later, Mark is there, holding my arm.

"Hey, hey, are you okay?"

I nod. Bile twists in my stomach. Every cell in my body had screamed out to turn around and run, all at once. Now that it's over, I feel shaken.

"Fine," I whisper.

"What did you see?" he asks.

"Nothing."

It's not a lie, but it feels like one.

His eyebrows furrow, but he doesn't press it.

"Come on," he says. "The sooner we find what you're looking for, the sooner this is all over."

With him still holding my arm, we navigate the ruins of the room as we head toward the back.

The house is a similar layout to Elizabeth's, only mirrored. And it's hard to explain, but with every step, I feel a hatred for Mr. Pierce grow. Like it's stained the entire house, and the closer we get to its heart, the worse it becomes.

"Can you sense that?" I ask Mark.

"Sense what?" he replies.

"This house . . . it feels angry."

"I suppose that makes sense. Mr. Pierce was really unhappy when he died."

"Because of Elizabeth and James?" I ask.

Mark looks at me strangely. "Yeah. How did you know?"

Sienna also gives me a look, though her expression is clear: *Don't tell him!* But I have to. We don't have much time left and keeping secrets isn't helping. Besides, he's seen Elizabeth's ghost.

"I have her journal," I admit.

Sienna groans and rolls her eyes, upset that I finally spilled.

"You do?" Mark asks. "How? Did you find it in her house?"

"It showed up on my porch, actually. A few days ago. That's why we came here. I'd been having visions of her for as long as I can remember, and when her journal showed up, I knew we had to solve what happened to her. I think she must have left it for me."

Mark's eyes are wide. I keep waiting for him to laugh. But instead, he nods gravely.

"That makes sense. I knew there was a deeper reason you came here. Did you learn anything else?"

I shake my head. "It just said that she and James played a prank on Mr. Pierce. And she said she was worried about someone coming after her." I shrug. "I figured it was Mr. Pierce, but maybe it was James?"

"Sounds like we need to interrogate James after all," Sienna says.

"I wouldn't," Mark replies.

"He might be our only lead."

"Maybe," Mark says. "But like I said, he doesn't talk much anymore. I know that he and Elizabeth had played a few pranks on Mr. Pierce before she died . . ."

"Do you think they did . . . this?" I ask, gesturing

around. I can't imagine Elizabeth breaking all this furniture, but who knows?

"I don't think so. I mean, I don't think I'm strong enough to break stuff like this, do you? No, this is an adult's work." He looks around, assessing the damage, then stares back at me. His gaze is intense. "Do you have the journal? Maybe there's more in there. Hints about what happened to her."

"Maybe," I admit. "The last few pages were torn out, though. Who knows what they said?"

Mark looks disappointed. I get it: another dead end.

"Well, I guess we search around here," he says. "Maybe we'll turn up clues."

"Lead the way," Sienna says.

Mark starts down the stairs to the basement. Sienna pulls me aside.

"I can't believe you told him everything!"

"What's it matter?" I ask. I look to his retreating back. "We're gone tomorrow and we still haven't learned anything. Secrets aren't helping."

"Secrets might have been the only things keeping us alive," she replies darkly.

"You really don't trust him?"

"I don't trust anyone who's this helpful for no reason. Which is why I can't wait to get out of this town.

Honestly, maybe we should leave tonight? There's a late bus we could take."

My gut squirms. I feel like we're so, so close to finding the answers. But at the same time, Elizabeth doesn't seem to *want* us to find the answers. Maybe Sienna's right. Maybe we should just leave, before anything bad happens. Or before we get more disappointed.

"What are you two talking about?" Mark calls back.

"Nothing!" Sienna says. She looks at me, daring me to speak. I stay silent as we hurry to catch up.

The basement . . . well, it's not that different from any other basement, really. There are storage boxes slouched with decay, shelves filled with canned goods that are way past their expiration. The only thing of any interest is a bookshelf along the far wall, filled with what looks like journals and newspaper clippings.

"Maybe there's something in here," Mark suggests.

"Great," Sienna says, throwing a look at me. "More reading. And not the fun kind."

Despite her grumbling, she goes over and joins Mark.

I slowly make my way over. But I don't go straight to the bookshelf. I feel a tug toward the wall, toward a glint in the pile of bricks that no one else seemed to see. For some reason, I don't flick my flashlight over that way—I pretend to be studying everything else, from the piles of cardboard boxes to the broken-down water heater tank. Then, pretending to stoop to tie my shoe, I investigate.

There's something in the pile of bricks, all right.

Something that looks like it had been hastily hidden.

I reach over . . . and find a key.

An old, rusty skeleton key.

The type that could unlock any door in this house. Or, potentially, Elizabeth's.

"Hey, look at this!" Sienna calls out, way too loudly. I jolt, nearly dropping the key, to see her pulling out an old photo album from the shelf.

I quickly pocket the key and hurry over.

"What is it?" I ask. I try not to reach into my pocket again to touch the key. For some reason, I don't want either of them to know about it.

Sienna shows the album to me. The three of us crowd around it.

It's filled with photographs of kids playing.

Of Elizabeth and James playing.

Instantly, a vision slams into me, and I stand outside Elizabeth's house while the two of them play in the yard. They toss a large ball back and forth. When

James gets it, he tosses it hard at Elizabeth, who starts to cry . . .

"What is this doing here?" Sienna asks.

I'm back in the basement, staring at the photos. Including one of James and Elizabeth, tossing a ball.

"I don't know," Mark says uneasily. "Like I said, Mr. Pierce wasn't a nice guy. Maybe he stole it from their house. Maybe he was watching them."

I shudder. I can't tell if it's fear or the aftereffects of the vision.

"Creepy," Sienna says. "But still doesn't help us."

She flips through the photo book, front to back. It's entirely made up of pictures of Elizabeth and James. Too creepy. Then she shoves it back onto the shelf with a sigh. "There's nothing else down here. And we're no closer to figuring out what really happened to Elizabeth, or how we're going to put her spirit to rest."

"Why don't we try upstairs? I bet there's something in one of the bedrooms."

"Let's try it," I say. "We're here. We should at least give it a shot."

"Fine," Sienna says. "But remember what I said."

She storms up the steps. Mark turns to me. "What did she say?"

"Nothing," I say. "She's just in a bad mood."

22

Mark grunts, then heads upstairs. I follow. I know Sienna wants to leave town, but I don't want to leave until I've tried out this skeleton key. I want to know what Elizabeth hid in her basement. It feels important.

We make our way upstairs. The bedrooms are in disarray, the beds molding and gross. No newspapers, no confession note. Nothing. After twenty minutes of searching, my head hurts from the bad smells and I'm starting to warm up to Sienna's idea. Maybe we should go home tonight.

If Elizabeth really wanted me to solve her death, she'd have been a little more helpful.

"This is pointless, isn't it?" Sienna asks. She's pulling clothes from the closet, searching pockets, while Mark pokes through the wardrobe and I shuffle through a small bookshelf.

"What do you mean?" Mark asks. "We're so close!"

"Are we, though? We haven't learned anything we didn't already know. Maybe we should just give up. Go home."

"But you can't!" Mark blurts. "What about Elizabeth? What about putting her soul to rest?"

"What about it?" Sienna asks. "Even if it *was* James or Mr. Pierce, what are we supposed to do about it? It was stupid of me to think we'd find what professionals couldn't." She looks at me. "What do you think, Kara? You're the one with the visions. Should we just go home? Tonight. I really don't want to stay another night in that house if I don't have to."

"Tonight?" I don't know why, but Mark looks frantic. "You can't leave *tonight*."

"Yeah we can," Sienna says. "There's a bus later this evening. Kara? You in?"

"I—" But before I can finish my sentence, Elizabeth answers for me.

"LEAVE NOW!"

Her words echo through the house, and I know it's no vision. I know because Sienna screams and Mark clasps his hands to his ears as the whole house goes haywire.

I yell out as photos drop from the walls and their

frames crash against the floor. Windows shatter, shards of glass flying out into the yard far below.

"Run!" I manage to cry out.

I don't see Elizabeth, but I feel her rage. We rush past the bathroom, and when I glance in, I see all the faucets spraying water. We hurry down the steps, and the very stairs buck beneath us like horses. I glance over my shoulder to see Sienna right behind me, Mark a few steps behind her.

"Hurry!" I yell.

I don't know why Elizabeth is so angry, why she wants us out so badly, but for the first time in my life, I'm terrified of her. My heart hammers in my throat as I leap past the armchair that's tossed against the wall, mere inches from my face. Curtains whip from their rods, snapping in an unfelt wind like ghosts or serpents, slashing at our faces. I bat them away.

I hurry toward the boarded-up window we slipped through, grateful it isn't covered in broken glass like the others. I leap through.

Panting, I reach in and grab Sienna's hand.

"Come on!" I panic.

She jumps through, landing on top of me. The porch rumbles under our feet, the planks thudding like thunder. We force ourselves to stand. I pull up the board and peer inside to see Mark struggling against a curtain that's wrapped around him tight.

"Mark!" I yell. I start to go back into the house, but Sienna holds me back. "What are you doing?" I ask her.

There's an anger in my voice that must frighten her, because she lets go. "Be careful," she says. I nod, ducking my head to go back into the house.

Elizabeth's face appears in the window, filled with rage.

"GO!" she screams, loud as a banshee. And with that scream comes a force that shoves me back. I skid along the porch and don't stop until I've tumbled into the grass. Sienna is right beside me.

"What was that?" she asks, frantic.

"Elizabeth," I reply. My head spins. "She pushed me away."

But why?

I try to take a step toward the house, but the force is still there, holding me back. It's like there's an invisible wall around Mr. Pierce's house, and there's no way to get past. Tears fill my eyes. All I wanted was to solve Elizabeth's death. Am I responsible for Mark's?

"We have to save him," I say.

"How?" Sienna asks. She slams her fists at the air, smacking against the same invisible wall. "We can't get through."

I stare at the house. It's gone completely silent. It

looks just like it did when we first came in: empty, deserted, sad. But now, I sense another aura around it: hunger. And a terrifying amount of anger.

"What about Mr. Hughes?" I ask.

"What about him?" she asks.

"Maybe he can help."

"You really think he'll believe that Mark was trapped in Mr. Pierce's house by a ghost?"

"I think he's the only one who might!" I say, frantic. "Come on, we have to hurry! Mark needs us."

I'm amazed, but Sienna doesn't refuse. With one quick glance back at Mr. Pierce's house, we run to the library.

23

We run all the way to the library, and even though it isn't far, we're both panting by the time we rush inside.

Mr. Hughes looks up from his desk in alarm.

"Kara. Sienna," he says, looking between the two of us. "What's wrong?"

"Can't . . . explain," I huff. "Come . . . quick."

Concern creases his brow. But thankfully, he doesn't stall or question. He just stands up and says, "Show me."

We hurry from the library. Even though it quickly becomes clear that Mr. Hughes could outrun us if he wanted to, he keeps pace with us and teases out the story.

"The ghost of Elizabeth?" he asks. "Really?"

I nod. I don't tell him about the visions, or the fact that I've seen her before. Because none of that makes sense now. Why was she so violent? What was she warning us from? If she just wanted us gone, why send me visions or her diary in the first place?

Finally, we make it to the house and pause on the sidewalk. I'm scared to take a step forward. I don't know what worries me more: that I might run into an invisible barricade, or that I won't and Mr. Hughes will think I'm making it up.

"This is it," I say. "He's trapped inside."

"What on earth were you three doing here in the first place?" Mr. Hughes asks.

"Looking for clues," I admit. I reach into my pocket, feeling the skeleton key I found in Mr. Pierce's basement. I don't even know if I want to see what it can unlock, not anymore. But it still feels important.

"But why here?"

"Because we think he's the one who killed her."

Mr. Hughes looks at me. "What?" he asks.

"Mr. Pierce," I say. I don't know why, but my words are frantic. "We think he killed her."

"Okay," he says. "But why did you go in there?" He nods toward the house.

My words falter.

Sienna picks up my slack. "We were told it was Mr. Pierce's house," she says slowly.

"I don't know who told you that," Mr. Hughes says. "Mr. Pierce's house is three blocks that way. And it's lived in by the Breyer family. This . . . Well, I don't know who lived here."

Mark was lying? Or did he just not know?

"What?" Sienna asks.

"It doesn't matter," I say. "He's still trapped in there. We still have to—"

"Hey, guys."

Mark's voice cuts off my frantic words. We all turn to see him crossing the street.

"Mark?" I say. "How did you . . . ?"

"Hey, Mr. Hughes," Mark says.

"Is this the young man who needed saving?" Mr. Hughes asks.

I can't answer. My mouth opens and closes like a fish.

"Sorry about that," Mark says. "I tripped and got stuck. But I'm okay! Clearly."

I can't speak. My brain is short-circuiting. Mark was trapped. Elizabeth had him. So why is he standing here, entirely calm, like nothing ever happened?

Mr. Hughes looks between the three of us kids, clearly confused. I swear I see him make eye contact with Mark—briefly—and it almost looks like he nods ever so slightly. But the movement is so faint I must have made it up.

"Well, I'm glad everyone's okay," Mr. Hughes says. "Though you girls look pretty shocked. How 'bout I buy you three dinner?"

"No," Sienna quickly says. "That's all right. Our . . . our parents are waiting."

"But—" Mark begins, but she cuts him off.

"It's fine! Just a big misunderstanding. We'll be going now."

"Do you want me to come with you?" Mark asks.

Sienna shakes her head. "No, gotta run. It's getting late. Bye!"

And without another word, she grabs my hand and begins to pull me away. I don't resist. I feel like I'm walking through a dream. I glance back once, to see Mark and Mr. Hughes still standing there. When they see me look, they both smile widely and wave. Shivers race down my spine.

When we're around the corner and out of sight, Sienna breaks into a jog.

"What's going on?" I ask. "Where are we going?"

"Out of this stupid town," she says. She glances at her watch. "We've got an hour before the last bus. We can make it. And then we're out of here."

"But what about our stuff?"

"Who cares?!" she asks, her voice hitching. A couple on the other side of the street smiles and waves at us. She lowers her voice. "Something really strange is going on and I don't want to stick around to find out what it is!"

She's right. Of course she's right. My brain frantically tries to put the pieces together but nothing fits, and right now, I don't care. I want out, too. All I want is to be home in my bed, with no more visions of Elizabeth and no threat of ever returning to this town.

We make it to the bus station with plenty of time to spare, but when Sienna goes to buy tickets, the attendant looks her up and down.

"I know you two," the attendant—a young man with curly blond hair—says. "Just got in yesterday, right? Why you leaving so soon?"

"We just are, okay?" Sienna asks. "It's none of your business. Now, two tickets for the last bus tonight. Thank you." She holds out some money for the fare.

I stare at her. I've never heard her talk so rudely to an adult before. But this time, I'm not about to tell her to be nice.

The attendant doesn't take her money. He doesn't even look at his computer. Instead, he raises an eyebrow, clearly suspicious.

"Sorry, kids," he finally says. "No can do. Last bus left a few hours ago."

"What?!" Sienna asks. "That can't be true! I just checked the timetable this morning!"

"Must've looked at the wrong timetable."

"No," she says. She reaches into her pocket. "Look, here—"

Her eyes widen. She reaches into another pocket. And another.

"What is it?" I ask.

"My phone!" she yelps. "I just had it! I must—" Her mouth gapes open. "It's still in the house."

She doesn't have to clarify which one.

"You know," the attendant starts to say, "the B and B in town could put you up for the night. Free of charge. Might even throw in a few extra days if you're lucky."

"We don't want to stay here another stupid day!" Sienna yells. "We want to leave!"

"Sorry, miss. Next bus isn't until . . ." He taps on the computer. "Not until Thursday, I'm afraid. You sure you don't want a place to stay?"

"No, that can't be real," Sienna says. She takes a step back, shaking her head. "You're lying. You're all lying!"

And with that, she takes off at a run.

I pause for only a moment, looking between her and the attendant. He smiles calmly at me. I want to scream.

Instead, I hurry after Sienna.

24

I catch up with her a block away. Mostly because she's stopped running; she sits on a park bench, head in her hands. I can't tell if she's crying or talking to herself or what. But I don't sit down next to her. I'm worried she'll bite my head off if I do.

"Are you okay?" I ask.

She looks up at me. There are tears in her eyes, but she doesn't seem sad. She seems angry.

"Of course I'm not okay!" she says. "We're stuck in this stupid town and I can't even call my parents to pick us up!" Her eyes narrow. "Wait, where's your phone?"

I reach into my pocket. My heart drops to my feet.

"It's not there," I whisper.

"What?" she asks.

"It must have fallen out in the house—" I begin, but she cuts me off.

"He stole it," she says.

"What?" I ask.

"He stole it!" Sienna yells. She pushes herself up to standing. "I knew it! I knew we couldn't trust him, but you just had to go and believe him, and now we're stuck here!"

"Me? Why are you blaming me?"

"Because you're the whole reason we got into this mess!"

Her outburst chills me worse than Elizabeth's ghost.

"You don't mean that," I whisper.

She must note the hurt in my voice, because she takes a deep breath.

"Sorry. It's just . . . I don't know what to do. We're trapped."

"Maybe we can get Mr. Hughes to give us a ride?"

"Are you kidding me? He's in on it, too!"

"No way."

"You heard him!" she exclaims. "All that talk about taking us to dinner, making us stay longer. Everyone in this town wants us to stay. Well, I'm not sticking around to find out why. I'm getting my phone back, and we're calling home and getting out of here."

She gets off the bench and begins storming away, leaving me no choice but to follow.

"But how do you know where to go?" I ask.

She pauses just long enough to look at me.

"Don't you get it?" she asks. "They want us to be stuck here. Which means he wants us to find him. I bet he's right where we left him."

I try to tell her that it's a terrible idea to walk straight toward a haunted house, but there's no point. I can tell from the look in her eyes that she won't listen to reason. She's angry. And—like me—she wants to go home.

x✗x

Halfway to the unknown, abandoned house, I get an idea.

Elizabeth's diary.

I reach into my pocket and pull out the skeleton key.

"What's that?" Sienna asks.

"A skeleton key," I say. "They open most doors in houses like these. I found it in the other house."

"And let me guess—you think it might unlock the door to Elizabeth's basement?"

"Maybe. Could be worth a shot."

Sienna sighs. "Well . . . it *is* on the way. But we aren't staying long. It's gonna get dark in a few hours, and I want to be out of this town by nightfall. Even if I have to walk."

I nod. I don't want to be here any longer than I have to, either.

✗✗✗

We hurry to Elizabeth's house and sneak inside. I keep expecting to see Mark hiding behind a sofa or something, but there's no one there. Not even a trace of Elizabeth.

"Weird," I whisper. "This place feels so empty."

She gives me a strange look. "It was empty when we got here."

"I know," I say. "But Elizabeth . . . I dunno, she's gone."

"Good. Let's hope she stays that way."

"But—"

"Look, I know we came here to learn what happened to her. But she scares me. The sooner we're out of her reach, the better."

I sigh.

"Yeah. I just wish I knew what was wrong. That Elizabeth we saw earlier . . . It's not the Elizabeth I've seen all these years."

"Well, maybe whatever's hidden in the basement will hold a clue."

She doesn't sound that hopeful, but I nod.

When we reach the basement door, I expect

another vision or apparition, but nothing happens. I pull out the key and place it in the lock, give it a hesitant twist.

The door opens.

Cold, dusty air spills out. Along with it, I hear Elizabeth's whispered voice:

"Hurry."

I can't tell if she's telling me to hurry into the basement, or hurry up and leave.

I turn on my flashlight and carefully descend.

Instantly, I'm reminded of my vision. My dream. Of Elizabeth racing down here, clutching something to her chest, tears spilling down her cheeks. She had hidden something down here. Something she hadn't wanted Mr. Pierce to find.

I know in my gut precisely what it was, too.

I head straight toward the far wall and press my hand to the brick, trying to find a catch or crack. Finally, after fumbling for a few seconds, a brick slides loose. I gasp in relief and pull it out. It falls to my feet. In the nook, bundled up tight, is a wad of paper.

But not just any paper.

I know even before I pull them out that I've found the missing few pages of Elizabeth's diary.

I take a deep breath and unfold the papers and

read them aloud, knowing that Sienna can't read the strange symbols that somehow only I can translate.

Jan 11

James is a monster.

I thought he would stop after our prank on Mr. Pierce. I felt so bad after. I watched Mr. Pierce crying as he cleaned up the egg from his house. I almost went and helped him. James told me not to.

James threattened me not to.

I didn't.

A week later, he wanted to pull another prank. He showed up at my house with a bunch of big rocks in his backpack. He wanted to go to Mr. Pierce's house at night and break all the windows.

I said no.

He said I had to, or he would tell everyone it was my idea to egg the house.

I had no choice. Last night, we broke the windows. After, I ran so fast I thought my heart would explode. When we got to a ssafe place, I started to cry.

James laffed.

He said he wanted to do more.

He said this was just the start. And I would have to help him. Or else.

Jan 14

I wish James would go away.

I tried to play sick but he found out. He got mad. He said I can't hide from him. Ever. He said he knows what I think. He knows I'm a chicken.

Last night, when I was asleep, he snuck in threw my window and scared me.

He made me make a promise.

A promise to never tell on him. Ever. No matter what.

He made me poke my finger with a pin. A blood promise. I had no choice.

I cried when I promised. He just grinned.

Jan 18

James is mean. Worse than I ever imagined.

He doesn't just want to prank Mr. Pierce. He wants to make his life mizrable.

I asked James why he hated Mr. Pierce so much. He said he didn't need a reason—Mr. Pierce just deserved it.

No one deserves what James...what we...did.

Last night, we snuck into Mr. Pierce's house. James brought spray paint. And we spraypainted all over Mr. Pierce's walls. We called him terrible names. Then we ran. I want to tell. I want this to stop. I want to leave this town and never look back.

But I can't. I can't. If I tell, James will make my life horrible.

I can never escape. I'm stuck with him. Forever. I have to remain nice to him.

All I can do is write this down in my diary.

I'm trapped.

Jan 19

Mr. Pierce is angry. So angry.

He screams at us when we walk past. He can't prove we've done anything, but he still screams. No one listens to him. No one cares. Not even the cops.

Now I understand why James chose Mr. Pierce—everyone in town hates him.

No one will come to his aid.

I have to.

I have to stop this.

I have to stop James.

Jan 22

James threatened me tonight.

I said I wouldn't join him. He wants to go at midnight to Mr. Pierce's house.

He wants to steal all of Mr. Pierce's pictures and throw them in the lake.

I said I wouldn't. Couldn't.

He said I would. Or he would kill me.

I don't know what to do.

I believe him.

And then, one final page, the final entry—the one that had been ripped in half. I open the diary and place it beside the old entry so I can read the whole thing.

Feb 10

He is coming after me. He is going to hurt me.

If you are reading this, I want you to know that it wasn't Mr. Pierce who killed me. It was James.

I know James is up to something. He is

so insistant on me coming to the lake. I don't think he wants to throw in the pictures. I think he wants to throw in me. So I can't tell his secret. Even though he knows I can't tell. Even though he knows I'll come back. If you find this, you need to know the truth: James is the monster. He must be stopped.

My chest burns when I stop reading. I flip over the pages, skim back through, hoping to find another clue. Hoping for it to make sense.

Mr. Pierce was never the monster. It was James all along.

Is that the house Mark led us into? Why? Had he messed up?

"I knew it was James," Sienna says.

"We should tell someone," I reply.

"Agreed. But we should do it when we're far, far away from here." She turns to go, then hesitates. "Wait, read that last passage again."

I do. Her eyebrows furrow.

"What did she mean by 'he knows I'll come back'?" she asks.

"I don't know," I admit. "Maybe she knew she'd come back as a ghost? I mean, she did come back, didn't she?"

"Maybe," Sienna says. "Come on. Before James finds us and turns us into ghosts ourselves."

We head back upstairs, Elizabeth's diary and all its missing secrets tucked safely under my arm.

We know the truth.

But somehow that truth makes even less sense than everything we'd come to believe.

25

We hurry all the way back to the unknown house. I swear it's not my imagination, but it feels like the whole town is out walking—people with dogs or strollers, joggers, bikers, even a couple walking a cat. They all stop and stare at us while we go. Some of them smile. Some of them wave. But it's their stares that make me shudder and move faster:

They all look hungry.

We slow when we reach the house. Will it even let us back in?

I don't have to worry—the moment I near the porch, the now-unboarded front door creaks open on squealing hinges. Inside, I see nothing but blackness.

"I guess that's for us," Sienna says.

"Yeah," I reply.

Every piece of me wants to run away. I almost turn around. Surely someone else should handle this. An adult.

But the diary grows warm in my hands, comforting, calming. As I take a step, my vision shifts.

"*It's dangerous to go in there,*" Elizabeth says.

I turn. She floats on the sidewalk beside me, staring at the house mournfully.

"I know," I say. "But we have to. It's the only way to get out of here."

"*You still don't understand,*" she says.

"So tell me," I reply.

"*I can't.*" She seems to struggle as she speaks. "*Just don't let him keep you here. No matter what happens, you have to leave.*"

"But what about you?"

She looks at me then, and there is such a deep sadness in her eyes.

"*The best thing you can do for both of us is to leave here. Immediately.*"

"Are you coming?" Sienna asks, snapping me from the vision.

"Yeah," I reply. "Let's go. But we have to hurry."

"Don't gotta tell me twice," she says.

We hurry to the front door.

Before we go inside, I look back. To see half the town standing on the sidewalk. Watching.

"I don't like this," I whisper to Sienna.

She glances back.

"Let's go," she says. She takes my hand, and together we enter into the house.

The house is eerily silent. The debris from earlier is strewn across the floor, but no planks or pillows rise to pummel me away. My feet creak on the floorboards, the only sound in the terrifying silence.

"Mark?" Sienna calls out. "Where are you?"

No answer. She takes a step toward the stairs.

"Come on, Mark. We know you're here. And we know you took our phones."

Again, no answer. At least, not at first.

Then a terrible cackle comes from upstairs. Masculine, deep, and definitely not Mark's.

"That's not Mark," I whisper.

Sienna's face is set.

"Whoever it is, I know they have our phones. And they can't take the two of us."

She takes my hand and squeezes. Despite everything, I feel a little warm knowing she's still by my side.

We make our way upstairs.

The trapdoor leading to the attic is open, the ladder down. Darkness seethes above us.

"You want your answers?" that cackling voice calls. "Come and get them."

Sienna and I exchange a glance.

"Who is that?" I whisper.

"We're about to find out."

With a grim determination, she begins to climb the ladder. I follow right behind.

The air in the attic is freezing and heavy. It presses down on me like a cold, wet blanket, wrapping me in complete darkness the moment I'm through the entry. As soon as my feet are off the ladder, the ladder snaps back up and the door slams shut with a large bang. I yelp and stumble into Sienna, dropping the diary to the floor. I can't see a thing.

I grab for my flashlight and flick it on, nearly screaming again when the ghosts of two girls appear in front of me.

No, not ghosts. Our reflections.

A standing mirror draped in cobwebs rests before us. I sweep my flashlight over the room. More mirrors are scattered about, as well as cardboard boxes and trunks and bags of old clothes.

"Mark?" Sienna calls, her voice much more timid. "Where are you? And where are our phones?"

"Right here," the terrible voice growls.

We turn around.

Mark.

He stands on the other side of the attic, and it takes me a moment to realize what's so strange—even though he stands in darkness, I can see him perfectly. Like he's glowing.

"Mark!" I say. "What's going on?"

"Are you really that stupid?" he asks, his voice angry and terrible. "Do I really have to spell it out for you?"

"Hey, don't talk to her like that!" Sienna snaps. "Just give us back our phones so we can go."

He smiles. It's not like the happy smiles I saw earlier. This one is twisted. Sharp. Mean.

"Oh, you're not going anywhere."

"Mark, this isn't funny," I say. "I thought you were our friend!"

He cackles. "Friend?! Please. This was all a trap. I knew I had to trick you into coming here. And the best way to do that was to play a helpful little mouse named Mark."

His words chill me. He was lying all along. But why? How did he know we were coming?

An idea forms, but it's too terrible to be true.

"Who are you?" I ask.

His smile widens. He doesn't answer with words. Instead, he grabs the standing mirror and angles it so I can see his reflection.

For a moment, it just looks like the boy I've known staring back.

Then my sight tilts, just a little, and it's no longer Mark at all.

It's the boy from my vision. The boy from the pictures.

"James?" I whisper.

"Bingo," he replies.

26

"But James is like . . . twenty-four years old," Sienna stammers. "You can't be him."

"Oh, but I am. I always have been, and always will be. You see, once you're born in this town, you never escape. Not even in death."

"I don't understand," I whisper.

"You would have thought she would have informed you better," Mark says, shaking his head. Then, louder, "You're not a very good ghost, are you, Elizabeth? I shouldn't be surprised. You weren't a very good friend, either."

"What are you talking about?" I ask.

"I can't leave this town. No one can. When you're born here, you're trapped. Sure, you can die—but you'll be reborn in another body. It's our curse. And for the most part, we've been content with it. It's a rather nice town, after all."

"Yeah," Sienna says. "So we've heard."

He glares at her. She shuts up.

"But what does that have to do with me? With Elizabeth?" I ask.

"Everything," he says. He takes a step toward me. I flinch back. "Elizabeth was my friend. My best friend. But she was a coward. She wanted to run away. From what she'd done. From this town. From *me*." He growls the last word, his voice taking on that terrible old burn. "She shouldn't have been able to. But that's where you come in."

"Me?"

"Yes, you. Your parents never told you, did they? That you weren't born in your hometown? You were born *here*."

I shake my head. "No, that can't be true. They would have said."

"Are you so sure? It was Mr. Pierce who told them, of course. When they moved here, pregnant with you. He came to them before you were born and told them the truth—that if you were born in this town, your soul would never escape. And they believed him! Can you believe it? They actually believed him."

"Why would he tell them?" Sienna asks. "If everyone loves it here so much, why would he tell them to leave?"

"Revenge. For what we did to him. Or else he was feeling trapped himself. I don't know."

"If he was reborn, why haven't you asked him?"

Mark smiles wickedly. "Oh, he didn't die. I lied to you about that. And many other things. He's locked away in the jail, where he can't ruin our little secret anymore."

"That's terrible," I whisper.

"No," he says. "Your parents leaving was terrible. They took her away from me. They took away my friend."

"I don't—" I begin, but a part of me is starting to understand.

"Your visions were never visions," he says. "They're memories. Elizabeth's memories. You were born the moment she died. In your parents' car. Just as they passed over the town's border. Not close enough to be trapped, but close enough for Elizabeth to escape."

I gasp. Sienna squeezes my hand.

"You killed Elizabeth?" I ask.

"No," he says. "Not on purpose. We were at the lake. Tossing in Mr. Pierce's photos. But she tripped. Fell in. I jumped in after, but she pulled me down with her. We both drowned that night. But only I came back within the town. Elizabeth found another ride." He looks at me meaningfully.

"No," Sienna says. "You're lying. Kara isn't Elizabeth. She's not."

"Oh, she's Kara. *And* Elizabeth." Mark leans in close. "Elizabeth's been hiding in her for all these years. I felt her out there. I knew I had to lure you here. So I sent you her diary, knowing you'd never turn down a mystery. But now it's time for the story to end."

"Then let us go," I say.

He shakes his head. "No," he replies. "I want my friend back."

"We don't—"

"If you're born in this town," he says, "your soul stays here." He looks between Sienna and me. "It's nothing personal, of course. But if I'm going to get Elizabeth back, well, her current host has to die."

"You won't hurt her," Sienna says.

"It's a means to an end," Mark replies. "And sadly, you'll have to go, too. Neither of you will be reborn here, of course, but that's a loss I'm willing to take. This is a great town. But it will be so much better without you here."

Mark smiles briefly.

Then he attacks.

27

Mark lunges toward me.

Sienna shoves me to the side just in time, but I drop my flashlight and Elizabeth's diary in the process. The flashlight blinks out.

Mark roars in frustration and turns his anger toward Sienna. I don't see it, but I hear him thundering across the attic, hear the crashing and banging as he shoves her against mirrors and moving boxes. Sienna calls out.

"Don't you hurt her!" I yell back.

Light flares in front of me. But it's not the flashlight.

It's the diary.

The pages glow with a pale, unearthly light. Pages flutter as if in a storm. Glowing fog curls up from the pages . . . and from that fog emerges Elizabeth.

"Elizabeth!" I gasp.

She looks at me.

"I'm sorry I didn't explain," she says. *"I couldn't. I*

tried, but we made a pact . . ." Her eyes squeeze. *"I wish you weren't dragged here. But I'll make this right. When I tell you to run, run. And don't look back."*

"But what about you?"

She smiles.

"Don't worry about me. There are worse places to be stuck. But I don't want you to be stuck here with me." She winks. Then she charges forward in a burst of light and smoke.

Mark yells out. Light flares in the attic, the whole room illuminated like a sunny afternoon.

Elizabeth slams against Mark, pushing him against the wall and away from Sienna, who's struggling to get up from the floor.

I rush over to her side.

"Sienna! Are you okay?"

She nods, panting, a hand to her head.

"He punched me!" she moans. "Can you believe that?"

"Come on," I say. "We gotta go."

"But our phones—"

"We don't need our phones! We'll find a pay phone somewhere. Somewhere far, far away from here."

Mark screams out. "No! You won't escape me! Not again!"

He lunges past Elizabeth and slams into me. The breath is pushed from my lungs as I skid along the floor.

"Elizabeth! Is! Mine!" he roars. He towers over me. I wince, look away . . . and see the diary at my side.

Right as he's about to strike, I grab the book and hold it before me like a shield.

Light flashes. A powerful force that knocks Mark clear across the room, where he crashes into a mirror.

Elizabeth appears beside me.

"Now! Run!"

Sienna grabs my hand and helps me to my feet. We rush to the attic door and push the ladder down.

When we get outside, the entire town is there. Watching. Behind us, light flashes in the attic. Mark yells while Elizabeth cries out again, *"Run!"*

We dart forward. The townsfolk are too shocked to run after us, or maybe it's some magic of Elizabeth's, because we run the entire way without anyone trying to catch us.

It's not until we pass the town's welcome sign that we start to slow down.

And it's not until we've walked another mile in the dark that I realize I've left Elizabeth's diary behind.

Hopefully, that's not the only thing we've left there.

Epilogue

"Are you sure you have to go?" Sienna asks.

We stand outside my house, by the moving van. My parents are inside, discussing the final arrangements with the movers.

"I'm sure," I reply. "It was their decision. They want to be as far away from here as possible."

Sienna sighs, but she doesn't fight. She knows that it's the smart thing to do, too.

It wasn't my idea to move towns. But then, it wasn't surprising, either. Sienna and I had barely made it a mile past Elizabeth's town before my parents showed up, frantic. We'd asked how they found us. Apparently, they started to worry that morning when I wasn't answering texts, and tracked my phone. They freaked when they learned where I was and drove over immediately.

They'd asked if I was okay, if anything had happened. And I told them the truth. About everything.

Then they told me the truth. About everything.

By the time we got home, they'd made up their minds—we were leaving. As soon as possible.

"Have you seen her again?" Sienna asks.

I shake my head. I haven't seen a hint of Elizabeth since leaving her town. Even though I'd wanted the visions to end, it makes me feel bad. I know she's trapped there. Again. But I also know there would have been no way of saving her. Not without losing myself and my friend in the process.

"Well, let's hope it stays that way," Sienna says. "I mean, I know it wasn't her fault, but still . . ."

"Yeah," I say. "I just hope she's okay."

"She will be," Sienna says. "After all, it's such a great town."

I laugh without humor. "I don't know if Mr. Pierce would agree."

"Probably not. Though hopefully they've let him out."

Hopefully. But even if he was freed from jail, he'll never be free of that place. It makes me terribly sad. My parents come out and say it's time to go. Tears fill my eyes. Sienna wipes away her own tears and then wraps me in a huge hug.

"I'll miss you," she says.

"I'll miss you, too," I reply. "But we'll be in touch."

"Always," she says. Then she grins. "We can send each other books in the mail."

"Deal," I reply. "So long as it's not a diary."

She laughs and sniffs, and we hug one more time. Then I follow my parents into the car, and we're off.

It feels strange, driving through the town, seeing everything that I thought was home for the last time. But it feels kind of good, too. I know we're heading toward a new start.

A new me.

One without ghosts, without visions. Without someone else's past in my thoughts. Heck, without Megan and her bully friends. Everything will be better out there. I know it.

Finally, we pass the welcome sign of my town and pass over to the next.

"Time for a new start," my mom says, smiling.

I smile, too.

But as I look out the window, I don't see just fields rushing past. I see my reflection.

And behind it, beside it, I see another face. Smiling.

I swear it looks like Mark.

ACKNOWLEDGMENTS

I am so incredibly grateful that I get to spend my days writing creepy tales for kids—it's like having Halloween every day!

I want to thank everyone at Scholastic for allowing me to write these chilling books, especially my editor, David Levithan, for his insight and Jana Haussmann and the entire Fairs team for their incredible enthusiasm. It's been such a life-changing experience working on these. Thanks to my agent, Brent Taylor, for his continued support. And to my friend and fellow author Will Taylor, for always lending an expert eye.

My deepest thanks to the countless librarians and educators who fight daily so their students can have access to the power of the written word. Your work is incredibly difficult, but it does not go unnoticed. Knowledge and reason will prevail. No stories should be hidden.

But mostly, my thanks go to you, dear reader, for loving these creepy tales and always asking for more. I can't wait to share even more scary stories with you . . . soon.

ABOUT THE AUTHOR

K. R. Alexander is the pseudonym for author Alex R. Kahler.

As K. R., he writes thrilling, chilling books for adventurous young readers. As Alex—his actual first name—he writes fantasy novels for adults and teens. In both cases, he loves writing fiction drawn from true-life experiences.

Alex has traveled the world collecting strange and fascinating tales, from the misty moors of Scotland to the humid jungles of Hawaii. He is always on the move, as he believes there is much more to life than what meets the eye. As of this writing, Seattle is currently home.

K. R.'s other books include *The Collector*, *The Collected*, *The Fear Zone*, *The Fear Zone 2*, *The Undrowned*, *Vacancy*, *Escape*, *Darkroom*, *Gallowgate*, *Last Laugh*, and the books in the Scare Me series. You can contact him at cursedlibrary.com.

Read more from

K. R. Alexander...

if you dare

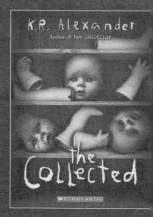
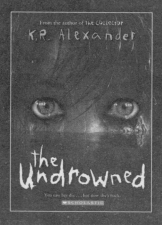

SCHOLASTIC and associated logos
are trademarks and/or registered
trademarks of Scholastic Inc.

SCHOLASTIC
scholastic.com

ALEXANDER-COLLECTOR